PENGUIN ᴅ.. .
YANGON DAYS

San Lin Tun is a poet, writer, lyricist, literary translator, literary guide, writing coach, and editor. He was a former short story instructor and literary translator of Hidden Words/Hidden Worlds short story project and a former coordinator-translator of My Yangon My Home, Yangon Art and Heritage Festival, and a former translator of Gothe Institute Yangon web page.

His writings appeared in local and international publications such as *Asia Literary Review*, *Borderless*, *Countercurrent*, *Global Poemic*, *Kitaab*, *Litehouse*, *Litterateur*, *Mad in Asia Pacific*, *Mekong Review*, *Myanmar Times*, *My Yangon Magazine*, *Myanmore*, *New Asian Writing Anthology* (NAW), *PIX*, *Ponder Savant*, *Pure Haiku*, *South East of Now*, *Strukturriss*, *Trouvaille*, and several others.

He was an editorial member of *Beyond Words*, Issue 5, a guest fiction editor of *Ambrosial Literary Garland* online magazine, a guest editor of *Open Leaf Press Review*, and a reader at Prism International.

His academic qualifications include a certificate in AmPox.3, a certificate in Start Writing Fiction, B.E. (Metallurgy), and M.A. (Buddha Dhamma). He is the first prize winner of Poetry of Wales National Day in 2015. His other keen interests are photography, playing guitar, and drawing cartoons.

His debut novel, *An English Writer*, is at Goodnovel, and he is now working on his second novel titled *A Classroom for Mr K.T.*

He lives in Yangon with his wife and two sons.

He can be reached at:
Facebook – https://www.facebook.com/san.lintun.12
LinkedIn – https://www.linkedin.com/in/san-lin-tun-3b67a050
Instagram – @sanlin855
Blog – www.writersanlintun.blogspot.com

ADVANCE PRAISE FOR *YANGON DAYS*

'A worthy successor to the stories of George Orwell and Somerset Maugham, the works in *Yangon Days* take us deeply into the lives of the residents of Myanmar. Each of the 26 stories is a highly evocative cinematic gem. If you are unable to visit in person, *Yangon Days* will take you there.'

—Mel Ulm,
editor of *The Reading Life*

'The inherently unique simplicity of both language and settings is mesmerizing, like a ball of pure white, soft silk cotton repeatedly caressing the skin of your face every time you open a page. San Lin Tun's characters are incredibly friendly and human. You become interested in the city of Yangon and the culture of Myanmar depicted in the stories, and your urge to actually see the scenery increases as you move to the next.'

—Jayanthi Sankar,
international award-winning author, Singapore

'Like a handcrafted lacquerware box containing precious rubies, sapphires and jade, *Yangon Days* is an evocative collection from one of Myanmar's emerging writers in English San Lin Tun. The stories subtly transport the reader into the extraordinary life and ordinary lives in the former Burmese capital, where everyday dilemmas and quirky observations reveal universal truths about loss, hope, and the human condition. Insightful and poignant, *Yangon Days* will resonate with anyone who has been enchanted by Myanmar.'

—Keith Lyons, co-author of *Opening up Hidden Burma* and contributing editor at *Borderless*

Yangon Days

A Collection of Urban Short Stories

San Lin Tun

PENGUIN BOOKS
An imprint of Penguin Random House

PENGUIN BOOKS

Penguin Books is an imprint of the Penguin Random House group of
companies whose addresses can be found at
global.penguinrandomhouse.com

Published by Penguin Random House SEA Pte Ltd
40 Penjuru Lane, #03-12, Block 2
Singapore 609216

Penguin
Random House
SEA

First published in Penguin Books by Penguin Random House SEA 2024

ISBN 9789815204797

Typeset in Garamond by MAP Systems, Bengaluru, India

www.penguin.sg

For my parents, teachers, especially Dr Bob Percival,
who loved Yangon and its streets

Contents

A New Transformer

When the two twenty-year-old urbanites, Myo and Soe, leave the movie theatre, they stroll down the street to a bus stop to take an uptown bus home. Myo is in a white shirt with a blue chequered *longyi* (men's sarong), while Soe is in a T-shirt and blue jeans. Myo is a bit taller than Soe, who is comparatively stocky.

Myo insists that they walk in the shade because he feels that the late afternoon sun, after their matinee show, is still very hot. Sauntering down the street, they animatedly discuss the movie, marvelling at the amazing settings and special effects. The sound system had been perfect.

Myo gushes, 'For a moment there, when the transformers battled with their enemies, I almost felt that I, along with my seat, had been tossed into the air. The drumbeat from the speakers was so loud because of the powerful Dolby surround-sound system. It was fantastic! So very different from any of the movies we watched in the past.'

He adds, 'You know, when the car in the movie tipped over and its wheel came off, the boy seated beside me shrieked in panic because he felt that the wheel had almost hit him.'

Soe nods, 'True. I, too, feel the rush . . . like I've just experienced the real thing—'

'We still have some free time, so let's watch the next movie. It'll be showing soon.'

* * *

Soe asked Myo to buy some packets of sunflower seeds and bottles of water so they could have something to munch on as they watched the movie. As always, there was a big crowd milling around the snack stalls that sold sunflower seeds, potato chips, bread, plums, and other small eats.

They walked up the carpeted stairs and showed their tickets to an usher who immediately guided them to their seats. They preferred the aisle seats because this meant they could go out easily without having to apologize to the entire row of people seated beside them.

They sat down in their seats in time to hear the stirring music of the theme song. It was really wonderful to listen to it. Then, the lights dimmed, making it difficult for those who came in late to find their seats.

During the national anthem, which was played before the movie started, Myo and Soe stood up to salute the national flag fluttering on the screen. The programme then went on to play the trailers for forthcoming movies. The young men looked around and noticed that the theatre was packed to capacity.

Some of Myo's friends said that they usually slept through movies because they found the atmosphere in the movie theatres very soporific. Some came to the movie theatre solely for the entertainment while some others liked enjoying a film in the company of their lovers or buddies. Some jokingly said that they preferred the lengthy Indian movies to the shorter western ones because they got to spend more time with their girlfriends in the cinema hall.

In reply to Myo's hearsay, Soe said, 'You know, I've heard my dad say that when we were young, we needed to pay only five or ten kyats to watch a movie. It's now two or three thousand kyats for a stall ticket; but I do feel that the movies these days are very good and worth it.'

* * *

As soon as the movie got over, people started to file out of the auditorium. Myo and Soe waited until most of the people vacated their seats before they got up and joined the slow-moving throng to the exit doors. They could hear people appreciating the movie.

Last Friday, Myo, who had been on a bus plying along Sule Pagoda Road, had looked out of the window and happened to see the large hoarding advertising the new movie, *Transformers*. He had immediately decided to invite his friend and hostel roommate, Soe, to watch it with him on Sunday for the matinee show after they returned from the magnificent and marvellous Shwedagon Pagoda.

Soe had promptly agreed. He knew that watching movies was good entertainment and helped him unwind.

It was a necessary stress release especially after a hard day in the office.

* * *

They stopped at the traffic light to cross a main road called Anawrahta Road (formerly known as Fraser Road). The road was busy at this hour. Myo grinned broadly at Soe as they waited for the stream of the cars to abate. And then, on a whim, Myo stepped out onto the asphalt street despite Soe's warning to wait until the traffic had stopped.

Myo saw the cab hurtling towards him and twisted away from the danger in the nick of time. It was almost like he believed that the speeding car was a 'transformer'. He definitely was still under the thrall of the movie. The alarmed people around him warned him to watch out and heaved a sigh of relief when he wasn't hit by the taxi.

Stepping hard on his brake, the taxi driver popped his head out of the window, 'Have you got a spare life, you moron?' and then followed up his question with a string of expletives, which Myo opted to take as a compliment. The taxi then sped off to beat the red traffic light.

Myo stood staring after the swiftly retreating taxi, his mind totally engulfed by images of autoboots and alien transformers. This was the second time he had watched the film. Mark Wahlberg was easily his all-time favourite actor.

He usually watched the movies of his favourite actors— Keanu Reeves, Morgan Freeman, Brad Pitt—because they rejuvenated his mind. He was bored by the sedentary, urban lifestyle: crowded shopping malls, crowded roads, crowded buses, and the flooding of streets whenever it rained. He loathed everything about city life. Watching movies was his stress buster and helped him escape into fantasy worlds.

This movie, *Transformers*, had made him feel like a whole other person, renewed and filled with entirely new concepts about the beginning of the world and the role of robots and aliens. To Myo, the message of the movie was that of the three dominant species in the world—the aliens, the robots, and the humans—only the robots and the humans could bring about peace and harmony on Earth.

Hollywood blockbusters were a huge, lucrative draw in the cinema halls. As an ardent movie-lover, Myo felt that all the trendy cars and trucks would someday transmogrify into the transformers, his heroes. He longed to possess robots of that kind in any place on earth. They would be truly powerful and invincible.

The theme of the movie was based on the timeless controversy: good versus evil. As always, good won through eventually and came out on top. With all the modern technology of computerized animation and special effects, the movie had kept the viewers fascinated, glued to their seats and on the edge of their seats, right up to the end. It transported each member of the audience into this fantasy world of transformers. Myo marvelled at the power of this medium of the silver screen. *What term could effectively encapsulate this phenomenon? Modern absurdity? Do we secretly yearn for a new order, or a new form of humanity?* These were his questions.

New ideas create a new world, but what we need is less problems. Hopefully the transformers would save the world, but it would come at a steep cost. There would be much destruction such as car crashes and burning buildings as portrayed in the film. We want peace sought out by humans not by robots.

* * *

Oh, no, no!

Soe noticed that Myo had become quite hysterical by this time, but Soe didn't quite know what to do.

Another sparkling saloon zipped past Myo, almost slamming into him. Myo remained motionless, believing that it was yet another transformer. Myo shook his head firmly to throw off these ridiculous notions induced by the movie.

He squeezed his eyes shut and yelled, 'Stop it! Get out of my thought stream.'

The people around them gaped at Myo in bewilderment.

Myo didn't know how to eradicate these crazy hallucinations. He stopped to look down at himself and gasped; his arm had solidified into hard metal. But even as he watched, it started to suddenly revert to flesh.

'Oh my God!' Myo gasped again. He realized that this was an unmistakable sign that he was going to turn into a robot soon and he could do nothing to stop the inevitable process. The change would be gradual and bit by bit he would become a robot. He wondered whether this would signify failure or success. He reckoned that some people would like the robotic lifestyle.

As for him, an artist at heart, he couldn't afford to become an emotionless robot. He needed to change back into a lover of beauty to survive in this life. He wished that the next time Hollywood decided to make a movie, they made one called

A New Transformer, which turned human beings into paintings, not robots.

* * *

Myo was in a daze when he regained consciousness. Soe told him that he had passed out after almost being hit by a speeding car. Thanks to the first aid administered by a kindly passer-by, Myo had recovered. Soe placed a supporting arm around him while people fanned him and provided shade with their umbrellas.

'You're very weak, which is why you fainted.'

'Everything is fine now.'

The crowd gradually dispersed as Myo sat up. He smiled and thanked Soe and everyone who had helped him. These were people with a good sense of responsibility and social consciousness.

* * *

High up in the sky, Myo could see clouds dissipating silently. Some birds were flying away as well. Soe smiled as he gave Myo a sip of orange juice to alleviate his dizziness. Myo was delighted to find that he hadn't transformed into a robot after all.

Days to Be Patient

An urbanite wishes that 'mind' could be included in the category of stretching exercises because he found several situations stressful—waiting for a bus forever, queuing up to buy tickets, and even standing at the fried-chicken food counters waiting to be served.

Crowded areas make him claustrophobic and he has often had to wait outside to avoid feeling suffocated. Remaining motionless, like a statue, would undoubtedly make him late to and from office, and his bad-tempered employer would tear a strip off him.

He gazes enviously at the carefree birds flying in the sky and wonders whether having wings would be the solution to all his problems.

* * *

One afternoon, during recess time, while enjoying a cup of tea with his colleague and best friend in a crowded downtown tea shop, he expounds this theory.

9

His friend laughs at the very idea, 'Come on, man! We need an inventor to "stretch" the mind. Where in the world can you find this genius? I don't want to see you bunged into a loony bin, so cut that crap. Just try to be patient. That's the best way to cope with your problems.' His buddy then turns away to dig into his delicious pea cake and tea.

As martyr to a fairly unique condition, he knows that very few would sympathize or empathize. In any case, he glares in frustration at his less-than-ideal, fair-weather friend, who is busy making short work of the cake.

He shakes his head resignedly and sighs deeply as he seeks a plausible solution to his conundrum. He finds it difficult to relax, or even think, in this sea of tea drinkers. He wonders why people talk so loudly in public places.

Unwilling to cause a rift, he does not rise to his friend's baiting. He takes a sip of his tea and then sets the teacup on the table sharply, losing his temper. This wasn't the tea he had ordered. He had asked for *poh-seint* (weak tea) but the inexperienced, young waiter had brought him *poh-kya* (strong tea). He controls the urge to fling the cup to the ground and tries to calm down.

He thinks, *What an incompetent waiter! He didn't take down my order properly. I need to teach him a lesson.*

He loathes poh-kya because it is too strong and invariably ruins his appetite, or worse, causes indigestion. He hails the useless waiter loudly and orders another cup of tea.

Bewildered, the waiter looks at him, 'Oh, didn't you order poh-kya?'

He shakes his head, 'I always order poh-seint, you nincompoop!'

Scratching his head, the chastised waiter disappears into the kitchen to fulfil the revised order for his nit-picking customer.

His friend bursts out laughing. His mirth evaporates as soon as he finds he's at the receiving end of a sour glance.

'I told you that we should go to another place. This place is so crowded that they mix up orders and are unable to cater to customers properly.'

His friend remains silent. Around them, the other customers merrily carry on with their loud conversations. They are 'talking teapots' he thinks—their mouths are the spouts of tea kettles—incessantly emitting steam. He chuckles to himself at the quaint imagery. He wipes the smile off his face when his friend scowls at him.

In the next tea shop, which is just as crowded as the first and manned by waiters who are just as young and inexperienced, they have to wait for a long time for their tea to arrive. The waiters move hither and thither taking orders from impatient customers. Depending on their personal preferences, people order various kinds of tea such as poh-seint, poh-kya, *cho-kya* (sweet and strong tea), *kya-sein* (even stronger tea), etc., therefore, it's quite easy for the young waiters to mix up the orders.

Tired of waiting for so long, he wants to go in search of yet another tea shop, but reluctantly sits down again because his friend insists that they have their tea at this renowned tea shop.

Our protagonist is cantankerous and when he gets impatient, his heartbeat becomes erratic, perspiration beads his forehead, his face suffuses, and he gets agitated. He has to roll up his sleeves and unbutton his top button to breathe.

Like a mantra, he silently and repeatedly recites the words: Be patient, be patient, be patient.

His friend notices this, but ignores him and continues to nibble on the snacks that have been served.

* * *

He invariably wants everything done quickly and hates to be kept waiting. His colleagues dubbed him with the sobriquet, 'Mr Short-Tempered'. He even broke up with his girlfriend who was fifteen minutes late for their date.

'A person who cannot respect time could never be my lover. I suggest we part ways forthwith.'

* * *

However, nowadays, he more than ever needs that special mental quality: patience. He knows that minerals like copper and gold have malleability and can be stretched. He has seen gold beaten into the desired shapes by the goldsmith. If 'mind' were pliant like these metals, it would be useful for all city dwellers, especially for our protagonist. Living in the city, commuting to and from office, he recites his standard mantra, sometimes audibly, sometimes not: Be patient. Be patient. Be patient.

Sometimes he wonders whether one's disposition is somehow related to one's horoscope and whether the stars reflect one's temperament. He's fairly sure that they are connected. If someone is born a Capricorn, they will be this or that, but most of them are invariably introverts. One doesn't need to go to an astrologer to confirm this.

However, people who believe in astrology will strongly object to such random generalization and it is entirely one's own prerogative to consult an astrologer. He envies those who are truly patient. He considers them exceptional. They never lose their composure even in crowded buses navigating the streets during rush hours, while others, impatient like himself, scramble to find seats as soon as they board the bus for fear that they will have to remain standing for the entire duration of the long journey.

On top of being impatient, he is an opportunist and does not wait for next time. No way. He knows that city life is transforming him, changing his way of life and attitude.

Look at him now.

He has been waiting in a very slow-moving queue to get sim cards for his newly bought handset. He scratches his head as he ponders his best course of action. He's busy in the afternoon and does not want to leave the queue and return later. Controlling his mind, he stands still.

In terms of Hla-Taw-Thar idioms, to have patience means that he will have to put his mind into a cane-juice wringer. It's his own hyperbole and he will be in trouble if Hla-Taw-Thar sues him for misquoting their name.

Nevertheless, he has also heard that the people in this village are good-hearted folk. (Thus, he offsets his acerbic remark with praise to ensure that he doesn't get sued.)

Long waits are a common phenomenon. When using the Internet, one has to wait while it buffers. At traffic lights, one has to wait. In a traffic jam, one has to wait, wait, wait, and then, wait some more.

Waiting has become a way of life. It is pointless to complain. Everyone has to wait for his or her turn to get things done. It is a pity because there is no gadget to stretch the mind and improve one's patience.

He looks at the long queue ahead of him. The seconds, with fully outstretched wings, fly quickly, but the mind is not being stretched. He knows his patience will soon run out with these interminable waits. In his mind he recites his oft-repeated mantra: Be patient, be patient, be patient. Yet again, he is not sure whether this mantra actually works.

Note: Hla Taw Thar is a place in Upper Myanmar and its people are well-known for their eloquence.

Mode of Transport as a Quark

Twenty-five-year-old Maung Hla, from lower Myanmar, came to Yangon to work after hearing the good tidings about the abundance of job opportunities in the city from his urban cousin Ko Tun.

Having gone to work in Yangon, Ko Tun had returned to the village a wealthy man, laden with gifts for his family and friends. He became the talk of the village. People wanted to hear all about his job and his lifestyle in the city, so he invited everybody to his house for lunch to satiate their curiosity.

He proudly announced, 'Yangon is big. So big. There are many tall buildings. As you know, there are also lots of pretty girls. Yangon women know how to beautify themselves. You will forget even the most beautiful village belles when you are in Yangon.'

Everybody burst out laughing, however, Maung Hla was paying close attention to his cousin's every word. The menfolk boisterously cheered him on upon hearing such provocative words, declaring that they wanted to see these marvels for themselves.

Maung Hla was solely interested in the business opportunities in Yangon. He was sick and tired of eking out a pittance in the village. He aimed high in life and aspired to be a Yangonite.

Ko Tun recommended, 'Don't stagnate here for all your life. If you want to improve your lifestyle, do as I did. Just look at how fine I am now. It's because I'm prospering in Yangon. Tell your parents that you want to come with me to work in Yangon. I will take care of everything for you. The only thing I need from you is your parent's permission.'

Upon hearing these words, Maung Hla tossed and turned in bed, pondering all night long until he dozed off just before dawn.

At 5.30 a.m., when he heard the cock crow, he got up, made his bed, and prepared for his morning devotional ritual. Reciting his morning prayers, he sprinkled water and lit candles in the shrine to Buddha in his home. Then, he prepared breakfast and recounted his cousin's stories of the wonders of city life to his parents. They heard him out patiently and then granted him permission to accompany Ko Tun to Yangon.

However, before he left for his cousin's house, his father said, 'Please bear two things in mind, son. Be honest and work hard. This is the only way to prosperity. As you know, I have lived my life with integrity. I've earned a good reputation and am highly respected in the village.'

His mother had tears in her eyes. He knew that she did not want him to live so far away.

She embraced him warmly, 'We are letting you go only because we love you so much and don't want to stand in the way of your dreams. Please live well and work hard in Yangon. Take care of your health, too, son, because I won't be there to take care of you. You'll have to learn to live on your own. Be friendly and don't fight with your friends. Can you promise me all that?'

He replied, 'I will, Mom. I will always bear your words in mind, and Dad's too.' He vowed to do his utmost to meet his father's high expectations and not let him down. He *shikoed* (paid his respects to) his parents.

Being a simple and straightforward man, he believed in honesty and hard work. He wanted to build his life on exalted notions of purity and perseverance.

* * *

As an old Myanmar saying goes, 'Unless you leave your comfort zone, you'll never know what fate has in store for you.'

Therefore, determined to live well as a result of his hard work in Yangon, he left his village for a better life. First, he needed to console his woebegone mother, who was very reluctant to let him go.

She asked, 'Son, how will you manage living away from me? You have never been to a big city like Yangon before. Who will take care of you?'

He reassured her, 'Don't worry, Mom. I will live with cousin Ko Tun and he will take care of me. He will even pick me up at the bus terminal. If I don't set out to seek my fortune now, I'll stagnate here like Father. I want to improve my life, Mom.'

After a thoughtful pause, she said, 'If you have made up your mind, I can't hold you back, son. Go and work there.' He saw tears welling up in his mother's eyes. He embraced her and repeated, 'Mom, please, don't worry. I'll take care of myself, I promise, and I will send you my earnings every month.'

She gazed into his eyes and said, 'I love you, dear. Be a good boy.' His father looked on silently at this touching scene.

* * *

At first, city life in Yangon felt strange to Maung Hla. Yangon was a great, big metropolis compared to his little village, which was devoid of any kind of public facility. He did not know how to commute on the public transportation buses and was clueless about Yangon's bus numbers and their routes.

In fact, Yangon had everything and he could have anything he wanted. He lived with his cousin Ko Tun, who was already comfortably settled in Yangon.

One day, to his delight, his cousin took him to the famous Theingyi Market. It was a shopper's dream come true. People milled around on shopping sprees. Every shop was crowded and it was obvious that businesses thrived in this city. The streets around that area were congested with vendors who called out their wares loudly to solicit buyers.

A charming salesgirl in a fabric shop beckoned to him to ask what he was looking for when he glanced at the displays in the shop.

'Hi, *ako* (dear brother), *mingalarpar* (auspiciousness to you). Can I tempt you to buy something for your girlfriend?'

He blushed hearing these words. In fact, he did not have any girlfriends yet. His cousin came to his rescue and pulled him away from the allure of the salesgirl. On the pavement, his cousin chided him, 'Try not to look stupid, gaping open-mouthed at things on display. Be smart when you are shopping. Those salesgirls are very good at conning dumb customers into buying things they don't really need.'

* * *

His cousin, who lived in a small house in a suburb of Hlaing Thar Yar township, promised to find him a job in the city centre. On weekends, his cousin brought him into the downtown area in the centre of the city to watch movies and eat at restaurants.

They hopped on a bus for this trip. Being a holiday that day, the bus wasn't too crowded, unlike on weekdays. It took them less than forty-five minutes to reach Sule Bus Stop. When they arrived at their destination, they disembarked along with the other passengers.

His cousin pointed out a tall building as a landmark, which Maung Hla later discovered was the famous Shangri-La Hotel.

Ko Tun explained, 'Before it became a hotel, it used to be a cinema hall called Pa-Pa-Win. I came here when I was very young to watch the movie *Superman*.'

Maung Hla listened attentively to his cousin's commentary and nodded.

He was amazed at his first glimpse of the magnificent, twenty-two-storey building. He also noticed that almost all the supermarkets were brightly and attractively lit but the items in the shops were exorbitant.

The fashionable Yangon girls looked angelically beautiful with the aid of all the cosmetics abundantly available.

He wished he could bring his childhood friends from the village to Yangon and flaunt the wonderful things here.

He also knew that, for a new arrival to the city, finding one's way around Yangon's streets and deciphering the bus routes were not easy and one could easily get lost. To an inexperienced person, all buses looked the same and it would be difficult to differentiate between Upper Block, Middle Block, and Lower Block in the downtown area.

Yangon had a grid pattern with numbered streets, starting from one to over a hundred. It had five major roads running parallel to Yangon River—Bogyoke Aung San Road, Anawrahta Road, Mahabandoola Road, Merchant Road, and Strand Road. Let's make an itinerary for a newcomer to Yangon:

First and foremost, if the person happened to be a Buddhist, they would want to pay their respects at the sacred Shwedagon Pagoda as soon as they set foot in Yangon. Not knowing which bus route to take, the person would probably decide to walk to the pagoda.

If they opted to take a chance on the bus and chose the route setting off from Theingyi Market, it would take them nearly thirty minutes to get to the southern stairway of the pagoda. En route, they would get to see the tombs of famous luminaries such as Queen Supayalat and Thakhin Ko Taw Hmaing.

Later, when he told his cousin about his expedition to the Shwedagon Pagoda from downtown, the latter cruelly dismissed his intrepidity as naive.

'You can hop on a bus from Sule Bus Stop or you can ask anyone in the street for directions to the pagoda.' His cousin's offhand remark was hurtful, but Maung Hla didn't take it to heart because he felt that it was more important to get to one's destination—whether one travelled by foot or took the bus was beside the point.

Ko Tun thoughtfully bought his young cousin a second-hand handset from a shop on Anawrahta Road as a birthday present, and then decided to teach him to use the Internet.

Looking at the beautiful red telephone, Maung Hla was delighted and thanked his cousin for his gift, 'Thanks, Ko Tun. You are a good cousin. I will always remember your kindness.'

Ko Tun felt so pleased by his cousin's gratitude that tears filled his eyes.

Soon afterwards, thanks to his cousin's unstinting efforts, Maung Hla learned to use the GPS on Google maps and then finding his way around town became a piece of cake. Already gifted with an eidetic memory, Maung Hla could memorize even the most difficult *Kiccayana Pali* grammar at his village monastery as a child. Therefore, he was a natural on the Internet and quickly learned to use it independently.

* * *

Strolling along the busy Strand Road with his cousin one evening, Maung Hla noticed some affluent citizens of the country riding on trishaws, enjoying the beauty of Pansodan Jetty and the sunset. They were in a group and seemed very happy. For locals, these were common enough sights, but for visitors, they appeared exotic and exciting.

Never having taken a ride on a trishaw before, Ko Tun felt that the new experience would be edifying and enjoyable for his cousin. Maung Hla unhesitatingly agreed.

They reminded him of the beautifully decorated oxen carts in his village, which were a joy to ride on to the village pagoda festival.

* * *

One Monday morning, after landing a job in a stationery shop in downtown Yangon, Maung Hla woke up to look at the clock that showed it was already fifteen minutes to eight.

He rubbed the sleep from his eyes with the back of his hand and exclaimed, 'Oh, no! Oh, no! Please, I can't be late.' He hurriedly rushed into the bathroom. This was actually his first day to work. He had stayed up late the previous night, watching the movie *Star Trek* on YouTube. He cursed himself under his breath for his carelessness.

He would be in the doghouse if he were to get fired on the very first day of his job. No way. His parents would be eagerly waiting to receive his first pay cheque. He had no time to lose, so he hopped into the shower, donned his work clothes, and had his breakfast at lightning speed before snatching up his bag and racing to the bus stop around the corner.

The bus stop thronged with people like him, waiting for a bus to get to work or school.

'Look, here comes one!' they yelled.

Get in. Stop pushing back there.

He knew he stood no chance of getting on the bus in such a melee. He glanced at his watch anxiously. It said half an hour to nine. Would he be in time, travelling all the way from Hlaing Thar Yar into downtown? He heaved several gusty sighs.

A new idea dawned on him like a miracle revealing itself. He knew that it was the only solution.

Perhaps he was obsessed by *Star Trek*'s teletransportation. He decided that all he needed to do was to visualize. Suddenly and unbelievably, he sensed himself being broken down into quarks and being teletransported directly into the office. He knew that that was what had actually happened—it hadn't been a dream or a figment of his fevered brain. It did happen.

He looked around and found the people beside him disintegrating into 'quarks' as well.

A Day on Which the Happiest Mind Rains

The weather has become quite unbearable. On the TV news channels, disasters like floods, storms, earthquakes, and volcanic eruptions are commonplace. These frequently occurring natural calamities are the direct result of global warming.

We no longer have three distinct seasons in Myanmar—summer, monsoon, and winter—because global warming plays havoc with the climate. When the seasons are affected by the rise in temperature, the rains come down unexpectedly.

Yangon is situated beside Yangon River, which causes a gentle breeze to blow through the town. The gridline pattern of Yangon streets allows an easy airflow and helps cool the urbanites. However, with global warming, Yangon's weather has become erratic—sunny one moment and rainy the next. Rain here, but not there. Rain there, but not here.

Even within the same city, people get sporadic rainfall. Who could have even predicted that the rain would suddenly come bucketing down in the middle of a scorching afternoon? People leave their umbrellas behind at home and end up getting soaked to the skin.

Freelancer Tun Myint is one among the city folk who experiences Yangon's volatile weather. He loathes the debilitating heatwaves produced by climate change. Because of his meagre income, he cannot afford the luxury of air conditioning at home. Whenever he feels hot, he fans himself with a rattan fan and lies down in the veranda on a *thinphyuu* (a rattan mattress—a natural product of the delta region).

Sometimes, his neighbours join him in the shade of the veranda, chatting desultorily and smoking cheroots. They sometimes make themselves *la-phet-thote* (picked-tea salad) along with a steaming pot of green tea. Crunching those chickpeas together with the peanuts makes the salad quite savoury, and adding dried shrimp powder simply enhances the amazing flavour of this hot afternoon treat.

On some humid days, Tun Myint reminisces about his village and his parents' spacious house with its huge courtyard filled with big trees such as *kokko* and *sein-ban* (jacaranda). When the sun rose high in the blue sky, he would just stroll down to the arbour beneath a tamarind tree and enjoy its refreshing coolness all afternoon into the late evening. The breeze eliminated the heat from the surroundings and the music of the leaves stirring in the wind was incredibly soothing.

Densely populated Yangon has no such luxuries. It has automobiles, buses, and other such vehicles in the streets. Some people can opt to go into an air-conditioned shopping mall. However, Tun Myint feels that the air in the shopping complexes is artificial and he prefers natural air to that of the AC.

* * *

Tun Myint graduated the previous year and currently works as a magazine illustrator.

At first he had found it difficult to find a job he liked, but later, through the connections of his teacher, he found paid employment in an established magazine as an illustrator and settled down into the city life, hoping for future success and distinction. This meant that he not only put his heart and soul metaphorically into the art world, he also put his limbs, his head, and his entire self into art.

He earns enough by illustrating for magazines and can send money, together with his magazines, to his parents back home. His income, fortunately, can sustain him with a good roof over his head and also puts food on the table. His parents are excellent moral support for the successful artist just starting out on his career. They do not want him to struggle to make ends meet as they had done, labouring all day in the fields with their pair of oxen. They know that a peasant's life is hard and want their son to live in the lap of luxury. They are confident that their son will become a famous artist someday. They are very proud of him.

Even during his school days, he drew pictures and sketches in his notebook whenever he had a chance. He always participated in the school's art competitions and even won prizes. His parents knew that they should support his hobby. Under the aegis of a village artist, who made paintings

for the village pagodas and monasteries, Tun Myint picked up
some rudimentary drawing skills.

* * *

Tun Myint rents a place in North Okkala Township with
a reasonable lease rate. He chose this place because he can
easily commute by bus to downtown Yangon. He shares his
lodgings with his friend who works in a garment factory. His
friend goes to work every morning, however, Tun Myint stays
home in the mornings and completes his illustrations before
submitting them to the magazine's office in the afternoon.
He goes downtown at around two o'clock in the afternoon and
meets up with his editor. He makes this trip thrice a week—
on Mondays, Wednesdays, and Fridays.

Apart from this, his friend, despite never having attended
a financial management course, showed him another way to
generate money to solve financial problems: pawning.

He knows that if he had done a management course, he
could have done so much more than just this and his efforts
to study would not have been in vain. It would be called
nānasampayutta citta (mind associated with wisdom).

It is very true that without proper past karma, one would
always be mired in poverty. Therefore, he believes that he
should work honestly, properly, and diligently. His motto
would be 'right livelihood'. These ethics have been inculcated
in him as a child. He wishes to build his life on good, strong
ethical values.

* * *

Three days ago, the editor-in-charge of the magazine summoned him to collect his remuneration from the office in downtown Yangon.

'Ko Tun Myint, can you come down to the office to collect your pay cheque? It will be ready for collection on Wednesday next week.'

On the appointed day, he gets ready to go to downtown to collect his money. He dons his favourite blue longyi and slings his Shan bag over his shoulder before leaving. Although the sun is merciless, he cannot take his old umbrella as it broke in a strong gust of wind the previous week. He discards it in the dustbin at the street corner.

He boards a bus heading downtown. It takes him forty minutes to get to Yone-Shin-Yon (cinema hall) bus stop near the Shangri-La Hotel. As he makes his way from the bus stop to the magazine's office, he notices that the streets are crowded despite the blistering heat of the sun. There are crowds at the cinema halls along the stretch of Sule Pagoda road.

He decides that, on the way home from the office, he would drop by at a store on Anawrahta Road (formerly known as Fraser Road) and buy himself a new umbrella. He quickens his steps towards the office. In the lobby of the apartment building where the magazine's office is situated, just as he jabs the elevator's third-floor button, a betel vendor calls out to him.

Tun Myint shakes his head at first, but then buys some as it will make an ideal gift for his editor who is addicted to betel leaf. When he enters the office, he sees people working at their desks. He smiles at a staff member who looks up from his computer.

He then enters the editor's room. The editor seems busy selecting manuscripts for the magazine's next issue. Tun Myint waits patiently until the editor looks up from his work. He notices the sunlight blazing through the open window and concludes that there will be no rain today. The editor eventually puts down his pen beside a sheaf of papers and glances up at him.

'Hi, Ko Tun Myint. You have arrived. How are you today?'

'I'm fine, *Sayar*. How are you? Are you busy getting the magazine ready to go to print?'

'Business as usual, you know,' he shrugs. 'Would you like a cup of tea?'

Without waiting for an answer, the editor signals to the office boy to fetch two cups of tea. The boy hares off to do his bidding. Leaning back in his chair, the editor hands a cheroot to Ko Tun Myint and lights it before lighting his own.

Enjoying the tea and cheroots, they discuss literary issues. The editor says, 'Ko Tun Myint, your illustrations have become popular. Most of our writers want you to illustrate their stories. Keep up the good work. I will give you a raise soon.'

Tun Myint feels elated to hear this. His hard work is paying off and his life will become better. He replies, 'I will always do my best, Sayar. Thank you for supporting me.'

They chat about this, that, and the other for quite a while. The friendly editor sympathizes with his cramped lifestyle in the city, in a small, rented apartment, unable to afford a house of his own. According to his watch, Ko Tun Myint realizes that he has spent more than forty minutes with his editor; his belly rumbles protestingly with pangs of hunger.

When the editor offers him another assignment for the next issue, Ko Tun Myint readily accepts it. He thanks the editor for his payment and the new project and bids him goodbye before he leaves the office.

He remembers that he needs to buy a new umbrella and stops at a store to buy it. It costs him 6,000 kyats. The Asahi-brand umbrella in his hand looks at him amiably. He looks back at it indifferently.

Then, out of the blue, the heavens burst and rain pelts down. Most of the people in the street run helter-skelter to find shelter and avoid getting soaked, but Ko Tun Myint stylishly unfurls the new umbrella. He casually saunters down the city's streets, watching as people dive into nearby tea shops or bus stops to protect themselves from the rain.

The downpour empties the streets and only a few daredevils, who do not give a fig about getting drenched, dare to walk in the deserted town. As he walks past a tea shop, a writer colleague hails him, inviting him to join him for a hot cup of tea. Tun Myint replies that he has just had tea at the magazine's office and walks on.

As he crosses the busy Sule Pagoda Road, he sees an old woman in rags, walking slowly ahead of him, shivering in the icy rain. He realizes that she must have forgotten to bring her umbrella. She seems to be about the same age as his mother.

He wonders what he can do to help her. He only has an umbrella. He hesitates for a minute, asking himself whether generosity was difficult. He wonders whether he should offer to accompany her to the place she wanted to go. And then wonders what she would do if it rained again on the morrow.

Suddenly he knows what he has to do. He hurries over to the old woman and generously gives her his new umbrella, 'Grandma, take this umbrella.'

The old woman looks blankly at him in surprise. Silently, he puts his umbrella into the old woman's gnarled hand and walks away. There are people around him. Some may have seen his selfless deed, some may not have seen it. It means nothing. He knows that he did the right thing. He feels quite happy in his heart.

He does not hear the old woman's gentle blessing, 'May you be healthy, prosperous, and safe from any dangers.'

Raindrops pelt down on him, but he is indifferent to their onslaught. He feels that this is his happiest moment in life, walking in the rain.

The drains sweep the rainwater away into the Yangon River along with many good stories of Yangon people, both present and past.

The Sapient Shopper

Weekends provide a window for people to go shopping. Out of curiosity or simply grabbing an opportunity to escape the daily grind of routine chores, they visit the attractive markets in their city, especially the ones that are well advertised.

These marketplaces are invariably crowded all the time. Shopping centres, or malls (as they are now called), have evolved recently. They are great tourist attractions as well as a paradise for compulsive shoppers.

It is such fun to browse through the array of goods displayed neatly and conveniently, especially for people who wheel trolleys down the aisles of merchandise. One of the best things about supermarkets is the powerful air conditioning installed for the comfort of their customers. They have become a haven for urbanites who want to escape the daytime heat of Yangon.

* * *

Lu Hla is enjoying a lazy, leisurely day, lounging on a settee and listening to the soothing music he loves, his eyes squeezed shut in enjoyment. It is a new album by an artist who is very popular among the youth. He is propped up against a pillow that he bought the previous day. The atmosphere around him always feels tranquil when he is immersed in music.

Lu Hla is meticulously neat and tidy. Visitors to his home always praise his impeccable housekeeping. The tasteful décor of his small living room lends it a spacious ambience. On the pristine, light-blue walls he has hung paintings by famous artists. Some are depictions of rural Myanmar scenes, and on the wall facing the settee are the Bagan pagoda paintings. He appreciates the exquisite brushstrokes of Myanmar artists and their unique style of drawing. There is also some modern art by the late Khin Maung Yin, one of the earliest forerunners of Myanmar's modern art scene. Lu Hla acquired one of his paintings from his friend, who was an art aficionado and partial to Khin Maung Yin's works.

Vintage posters of Myanmar add to the beauty of the interior decoration as do the rare curios placed on display stands here and there. His Yamaha hollow guitar leaning casually against the wall in a corner adds a touch of whimsy to the whole ensemble.

As he is lost in his music, the telephone rings, startling him from his reverie. He quickly sits up to answer it. It is Thinzar, his girlfriend. She excitedly announces that she will be there in fifteen minutes.

After hanging up, he laments, 'Alas! Why on earth does she want to come here at this hour?'

They met just the previous evening when she coaxed and cajoled him into accompanying her to Bogyoke Aung

San market (formerly known as Scott market), saying she needed to buy clothes for herself and rattan wares for her friend.

He had to wait for her at the entrance of the marketplace for nearly thirty minutes before she eventually arrived in a taxi. She had brought along a colleague from her office on this impromptu shopping trip. Then she made Lu Hla pay the cabdriver.

Thinzar was in a pink blouse and had done up her beautiful hair in an updo. With a fair-complexion, she looked fabulous and he could not keep his eyes off her. She noticed this and teased him, 'Stop staring, Ko Hla. Your eyeballs will pop right out of their sockets. Is this the first time you're seeing me in this outfit?'

He looked away, embarrassed, and tried to focus on something else.

She chuckled at his discomposure and said reassuringly, 'Don't worry! If you get bored, you can wait for us outside. We'll be with you in a few moments.'

He nodded and went out. He sat down on a wooden bench on the sidewalk. He killed time doing some mental arithmetic and watching passers-by. He fortunately found a journal that carried an interesting article about a successful businessman. After a while, he looked at his wristwatch and realized that his girlfriend and her friend had been gone for more than thirty minutes.

Suddenly they emerged from Ward II (another section of the market). They beamed from ear to ear as they hurried over to him. They had managed to find everything they needed.

Thinzar looked happy and excited because she had got what she wanted. After all the shopping, she had worked up an appetite and asked Lu Hla to buy them Shan noodles at the food centre in the market. They walked down the main aisle and turned left to enter the section with the food stalls. She stopped at the noodle shop and ordered a Shan noodle for herself and *tofu nwe* (noodle with warm bean syrup) for her friend. He ordered a plate of noodles for himself. They all ate with gusto, and then he paid the bill.

After the meal, Thinzar dropped off her friend at a bus stop nearby and then told him that she did not want to go back home just yet because she wanted to check out some new fabric. He couldn't for the life of him understand the obsession that girls had with shopping.

The marketplace was full of tourists—Thais, Chinese, and people from many other foreign countries. The Thai tourists were interested in some of the Myanmar products such as Instant Myanmar Teamix, Myanmar thanakka, etc. The Western foreigners converged around the shops that sold precious gems to check the quality of Myanmar's gems and jade. They seemed quite happy to see them.

Thinzar took him to the fabric section and he was left to kick his heels for another forty-five minutes while his girlfriend selected cloth to be tailored into a dress for herself. She came over several times to show the material to him and ask his opinion about the colour. He patiently answered her questions to avoid incurring her wrath. Then, they had some more noodles at the stall before they returned home.

They usually shopped for new things at the malls. Both of them liked trendy clothes. Sometimes, she bought him reasonably priced shirts and, to return the favour, he would buy her a new blouse when he received his pay cheque. Window-shopping was taboo for him, but not for her. She got a huge kick out of browsing new stuff in the shopping centres.

Her happiness being his topmost priority in life, he always accompanied her on her shopping sprees—it was as simple as that.

* * *

Fifteen minutes after her call, the bell rings. He answers the door and finds Thinzar standing there. She exclaims, 'Oh, you lazy brat, why aren't you ready yet? Go and put on your shirt.' Thinzar is quite bossy, but a man in love is tantamount to a slave.

'Come on, Thinzar,' Lu Hla protests mildly, 'can't this wait? I'm enjoying my music. Okay, okay, just give me a few minutes to get dressed. Wait here for me, I will be back soon, all right?'

She casts a furtive glance at him, knowing his penchant for tardiness, and waits for more than a few minutes. She picks up the headphones lying beside a DVD player to listen to the music he had been listening to. However, as she is anxious to set off on her shopping binge, she cannot concentrate on the music. She wonders whether she would have to drag him out of his room.

Just then, he emerges from his bedroom, pulling on a blue T-shirt over his blue jeans. Thinzar surveys him critically, 'You always wear the same clothes. Why don't you have a makeover and change your image? People will start imagining that you have only one outfit.'

He knows that she is just teasing him, so he does not take her remarks to heart and merely grins. 'I didn't want to keep you waiting. I know that you're in a hurry to get to the shops.'

She loops her arm through his and they both go out. He locks up after them.

* * *

They hail a cab from the corner of the street because she is in a hurry. She chatters incessantly throughout the ride.

'You know, there is a discount sale at Ga Mone Pwint Shopping Centre. I really need new slippers. My old slippers, you see, are worn out on top of being so outdated. You know how much I love this brand . . . blah . . . blah . . . blah . . .'

Under the barrage of words, Lu Hla can't even think straight and sits silently. The cabbie catches his eye in the rear-view mirror and smiles sympathetically.

* * *

They arrive at the shopping centre in less than twenty minutes to see crowds thronging at the entrance. There is probably a big sales promotion going because they can hear loud music in the background. People are standing around watching as some youngsters put up a dance performance on the floor. A gorgeous woman vocalist is crooning on the stage and her fans are cheering her on.

Lu Hla wants to watch the performance but Thinzar hauls him away, 'Please watch it later, A-ko. If we're late for the sale, everything will get sold out.'

Thinzar drags him and they almost run up to the first floor where the discount sales are being held. He can't even ask her to calm down or slow down because he knows that Thinzar is a compulsive shopaholic, nevertheless he tries, 'Wait, Thinzar.'

He wonders why people are so obsessed with discount sale, seasonal sale, special promotional sale, and every other kind of sale. Whenever a festival approaches, they hold umpteen number of 'special discount' sales and people flock to the venue in droves to buy stuff.

He wonders whether it is a contagion by some unknown retail bug that renders people unable to resist the allure of the shopping centres. This in turn triggers a shopping spree en masse. He knows that some people are shopaholics. His girlfriend, Thinzar, belongs to this category and gives flimsy justifications for buying things.

'You know these shoes are usually so much more expensive—about 35,000 MMK for the pair. Today it's only 25,000 MMK for brand new ones. That's incredibly cheap.'

Her pretty face is pink with enthusiasm and her eyes sparkle. Her animation makes her even more beautiful. He finds her utterly enchanting and is entirely under her spell like a rabbit caught in the headlights of a car. *Poor man!*

But who will pay for the slippers? He . . . who else? It is the onus of love. *No. No. No.* It is the privilege of love. He happily pays for her purchases at the counter. He looks at Thinzar, who smiles at him sweetly and he sees a flicker of love in her eyes. She links her arm with his, proud of her magnanimous boyfriend.

* * *

With a brown paper bag tucked triumphantly under her arm, she holds his hand with pride. They are relaxed now after the marathon at the mall and filled with a sense of achievement. It demonstrates the extent of his love for her; an intimacy even. She deserves it.

It is done and dusted for now, but what about the next time the shopping bug bites her? Would they have to go through this excruciating exercise all over again? Maybe!?

'Ko Hla, my friends tell me that online stores are mushrooming all over the Internet,' says Thinza. 'I think I'll just browse the net the next time I need something and do my shopping from the comfort of our home without going all the way to the supermarkets through the horrid traffic and crowds. We simply have to choose the things we want and they'll deliver them to us. That's so convenient. I love the idea. What will you buy for me next?'

These wonderful words render him speechless with joy, so he merely nods. He sighs resignedly as he visualizes the dwindling stack of money in his account. Thinza notices this.

'I don't have a credit card, Ko Hla. Can you apply for one on my behalf?' Everybody knows that a winsome smile can melt ice, so how can a mere mortal resist a gorgeous woman's blandishments? He nods again.

6

The Curious Incident
of a Job Trainee

Doing business is not easy. It needs skills and expertise to be successful. One needs to understand both marketing strategy and demand. Some, however, say that the essential thing in business is location. Business-minded and savvy people tend to make money easily because they know, or they can predict, demand.

* * *

Seated in a library, Nyi Nyi Min thinks about his friend, Moe Lwin, who recently completed a course in business management.

'Moe Lwin is level-headed,' he reflects, 'he knows what does and does not matter in life. He pursues education. I have to be like him and study hard.' He envies Moe Lwin who is of the same age as Nyi Nyi Min. Moe Lwin had exhorted him to do a course in business education before starting up a business of his own.

Nyi Nyi Min looks at the books spread out on the table in front of him. He knows that he needs to spend more time in the library rather than in a tea shop. He decides to avoid his wastrel friends, who have a devil-may-care attitude about their future and just wing it through life. Unwilling to work or do something useful with their lives, they squander their precious time gossiping at tea shops.

One day, when one of his layabout friends telephones to invite him to a restaurant, he gives a flimsy excuse about needing to run an errand for his mother and refuses. His mother ran a grocery shop at home, selling commodities like rice, oil, salt, onions, etc. He helped her whenever he was free or before he left for college.

When Nyi Nyi Min advises his friends to think about their future and plan a career, they taunt him with labels like 'Big Boss' behind his back. Nyi Nyi Min is understandably hurt when he learns of this from one of his closest friends. He feels that they misunderstood his well-intentioned advice.

Having seen many youngsters fritter away their precious youth fraternizing in cafeterias rather than studying in a library, he knows that he needs to spend his time more efficiently, especially with life becoming very competitive because of the constantly changing technology. He needs to keep up with the technological advances to avoid being left behind. He comes often to the library to read as many books as he can without dilly-dallying.

He loves to read about sales and marketing. The public library, on the second floor of a tall building in downtown Yangon, has tons of books and is a haven for him.

* * *

'Nyi Nyi, you have to enrol in a business management class before you start your own business. These days small businesses are so promising and some of them are really thriving,' Moe Lwin had said earnestly.

He truly meant it, because they had seen some very successful small-business owners showcasing their booths at the fair in the famous Yangon Park. People showed a lot of interest in their products. People these days prefer to invest in quality products rather than cheap goods.

* * *

Finally, after seeing an advertisement in the newspaper for a business school with an impressive alumni and reading up on their success stories, Nyi Nyi enrolled in one of the schools in downtown Yangon. Classes had already begun the previous month.

* * *

Moe Lwin is not only knowledgeable about setting up a business and building a company profile, but he also has an excellent understanding of everything one needs to do business. Nyi Nyi Min, however, wants to become a successful salesperson before he becomes a marketing guru. He envies the life of a salesperson who gets to travel a lot, selling his products in town after town.

'What an adventurous life!' he reflects. The very thought makes him happy. He would visit as many places as he likes around Yangon as well as in all of Myanmar. He would lead an exciting and full life. Nevertheless, as a down-to-earth person, he knows how very different reality is from fantasy. It is true, he is clueless about how hard a salesperson's life is—the amount of effort it takes to sell products or deal with difficult customers.

* * *

It has been two months since Nyi Nyi Min completed his business course, but he is yet to land his dream job. He needs a job urgently because he does not want to depend on his parents any longer, but his meagre bank balance is depleting rapidly and no income is in sight.

One day, out of frustration, Nyi Nyi Min telephones Moe Lwin and tells him about his predicament.

Moe Lwin replies, 'Don't worry, buddy. I will tell my uncle about you. He is in the publishing business and wants good salespeople for his recently opened bookshop in Hle-Dan, which is quite close to Yangon University. As you know, that place is teeming with students. There are plenty of hostels around that area and the idea to establish a bookshop there was a stroke of genius. Anyway, I will call you later and let you know.'

Moe Lwin is a truly good friend to offer to find him a job in Nyi Nyi's time of need.

* * *

On the appointed day, Nyi Nyi Min arrives in a spotless white, collarless shirt and a blue-chequered longyi. Not only does he have a good personality, he also looks dapper and energetic. Moe Lwin introduces Nyi Nyi to his uncle, U Soe, at the publishing company.

They remain standing politely until U Soe bids them sit down. His friend makes the introduction, 'U Soe, this is my friend, Nyi Nyi. He wants to work in your bookshop. He recently completed his business course.'

'Nice to meet you, Nyi Nyi.'

Nyi Nyi replies in kind. U Soe had seen some promising features in Nyi Nyi Min even before interviewing him. Although he discovers that Nyi Nyi Min is a complete novice in the field of sales, U Soe liked to encourage youngsters who were willing and eager to work and agrees to hire Nyi Nyi as a salesperson in his bookshop.

Nyi Nyi Min is delighted when he is asked to start work on the following Monday. He makes a mental note to call his mother and give her the good news.

After they say goodbye to U Soe, Moe Lwin and Nyi Nyi stroll down to the bus stop. Moe Lwin suggests they celebrate.

'We can stop at a café near the bus stop and have some snacks . . . my treat.'

Nyi Nyi Min agrees. At the café, they order some cold drinks and sandwiches. While they wait for their order, Nyi Nyi Min thanks his friend again. He assures him that he will not let him down and will do his utmost to justify his position in the bookshop.

His friend replies, 'I believe you, Nyi Nyi. Go on, tuck in. You seem thirsty after the interview.'

Nyi Nyi Min could not help smiling.

* * *

When he arrives at the bookshop on his first day, U Soe takes him under his wing and shows him the ropes. Nyi Nyi Min needed a few weeks of training in salesmanship. The purpose was to learn about the products he had to sell. There were different categories in the bookshop—fiction, non-fiction, self-help, history, languages, religion, textbooks, and so on.

U Soe encourages Nyi Nyi and is supportive whenever he has any difficulties distinguishing the category of a specific book. Soon Nyi Nyi Min becomes quite adept in identifying the various classifications of the books. He makes mental notes of everything. He sees a bright future for himself. He knows that luck is not sedentary; it is dynamic. To be a good salesperson he needs good communication and interpersonal skills in addition to having a pleasant personality.

He tries to read as many books as possible on salesmanship to improve his knowledge base. It really pays off. The company sends him to one of their outlets in a major shopping centre as an intern.

* * *

He is tasked with taking care of a book counter. Whenever customers come in, it is his job to help them find the books they want. He leads them into the aisles of books. Sometimes, it is fairly easy to find the book they need, but not all the time. He has to be patient until he locates the right book.

The stern-faced manager likes him because he is diligent and shows a keen interest in the business. The company plans to hold an annual book-sale event, which is a hectic time for all the employees.

Nyi Nyi Min is put in charge of book display and arrangements. He places the new publications in the forefront and prominently showcases their list of bestsellers on the message board. He understands that there are many genres in literature: biographies, novels, memoirs, short stories, fiction, non-fiction, and so on.

He feels that their sales could be outstanding. If their proprietor is happy, there is a good chance that he will be rewarded for good salesmanship. It is an excellent opportunity for him to display his skill and creativity.

* * *

Somebody thumps his shoulder and breaks his pleasant daydream. He turns around to identify the intruder and finds himself facing a male customer asking him to locate a book that he desperately needs.

He is surprised because the person before him is none other than his old classmate, Myo Gyi, who also recognizes him instantly.

Myo Gyi seems to be in a rush. Out of curiosity, Nyi Nyi Min asks, 'Why are you in such a hurry, buddy? What are you looking for?'

Breathlessly, Myo Gyi says, 'Hi, Nyi Nyi. I'm looking for a guidebook to help me become instantly taller. I need it desperately 'cos I need to apply for the job I have had my eye on for quite some time. Do you happen to have such a handbook?'

This intrigues Nyi Nyi and he wonders about the position his friend has sought. It sounds quite unique. He lets the enthusiastic job seeker explain it to him.

'You see, it is a very significant job and not everybody can apply for it . . . not even a person with a doctorate.'

Nyi Nyi Min finds this mind-boggling. He feels that Myo Gyi is probably exaggerating and wonders, 'Just what kind of a job is this? Is it something like the verger's job in Somerset Maugham's short story in which a verger, who is forced to leave his job because of his illiteracy, goes on to make a killing in business and becomes rich beyond his dreams. He reflects upon what his fate would have been had he not been kicked out of his job as a verger in the church. The answer was, ironically, he had to be an educated person to be a verger.'

He listens to his classmate's clarification, 'You see, Nyi Nyi, I desperately need this job, but—'

'What kind of a job is this?' demands Nyi Nyi impatiently.

With eyes that looked disdainfully at Nyi Nyi Min's naiveté, Myo Gyi exclaims, 'It is a trendy job popularized by Hollywood movies. It is a personal security job that needs the applicant to be more than six feet tall. Now, I am five feet and seven inches. That is why I need a "get taller instantly" book. Will you help me to find one, Nyi Nyi?'

At last, Nyi Nyi Min has his answer. Words fail him as he realizes just how demanding his new job is.

The Confessions of a Bridegroom
as a Wedding Planner

Myo and five of his collegemates are at a café, chatting about their lives and businesses. After their graduation, these friends had each gone their separate ways to tend to their own businesses and had not met each other in ages. When they decide to get together, it is Myo who moots the idea of meeting up here, at this café.

He is the first to arrive at the rendezvous and has to wait for about fifteen minutes for the rest of the group. Looking around the room, he sees some of his work colleagues at a table and they wave to him, inviting him to sit with them. Myo declines their offer, saying he is here to meet his old friends and that they would arrive soon.

A few minutes later, his friends stroll into the café. They look as light-hearted and carefree as ever. Myo seems to be the only one in the group lumbered with duties and responsibilities because he is a married man. As always, unmarried men want information about married life and

Myo, being the only experienced man, has to face a barrage of questions.

They pull his leg, 'Myo, why are you in such drab clothes? You should wear fancy togs, man. Doesn't your wife buy you trendy stuff?'

Myo knows that they are merely teasing and responds to their badinage, 'No. I just want to be Myo. I don't want to upgrade my wardrobe just because I'm married.'

One of them asks, 'Myo, why did you not bring your wife here to meet us? Are you trying the bachelor life for a change?'

Another friend jokes, 'I'll call your wife and tell her you are behaving like a bachelor and flirting with other girls. Haha!

He understands that the kidding is all in good spirit and he does not hold it against them. He pretends to be henpecked and says, 'Don't say that, guys! You don't know how jealous and possessive my wife is. She never lets me even speak to other women. Just goes to show how much she loves me.'

His friends guffaw heartily. Then, another friend asks, 'Hey, I want to know how you and your wife make up when you squabble. Who calls first—you or your wife?'

Myo replies with a straight face, 'I never make the first move to reconcile. I wait for her to speak to me instead.' His friend seems satisfied with his response and grins.

A couple of the guys, who are bridegrooms-to-be, ask, 'Hey, Myo, tell us about your experience in arranging a wedding. How did you cope?'

Intending to tease them in retaliation, Myo replies enigmatically, 'It's quite easy if you have a wedding planner, otherwise you will face a dilemma when you try to arrange your own marriage. In my case, I had to plan the whole thing from scratch, four or five months in advance, before the wedding.'

Everyone grows sombre when they hear Myo's answer. Murmurs arise among them as they exchange worried glances.

Someone raises his finger, 'Really? How come? Can you share your experience? It doesn't matter whether it is good or bad. We can all pick up some handy tips from your experience. If it is too difficult, I will opt to remain a bachelor.'

One of the guys expresses his reservations about marriage. Myo is worried that, with such a bleak outlook about marriage, this friend could really end up alone and without the enjoyable companionship of a wife. In fact, a wedding only needs proper management to be a joyful occasion—if not, it could become a series of disasters.

Another friend, who seems to be a confirmed bachelor and has been silent all this while, exclaims, 'That's exactly why I prefer to stay single. I am an introvert and self-conscious about standing up in front of people.'

No one argues with this as they unanimously agree that everybody has a right to their individual point of view, and that everyone's opinions and suggestions should be heard and respected. However, this speaker's tone conveys a disheartening sense of failure to the entire group at the table and so, although they say nothing, they roll their eyes in exasperation at his defeatist attitude.

They know that at this rate he won't be able find his soulmate. They also feel that, if he had ever had a girlfriend, his timidity would have driven her into the arms of another man.

Another friend cuts in, 'I love my girlfriend so much that I will try to convince her to elope with me if her mom does not agree to our marriage. My motto is: all is fair in love and war. I believe that love operates on a first come, first served basis. I do not believe in platonic love.'

However, Myo does not agree with such macho sentiments. He prefers the propriety of formally asking the parents for their daughter's hand—a tradition, he feels, one ought to preserve. He would need her parents' consent to ensure that the course of their married life remained smooth. It would be impossible for the newly-weds to be happy if their respective parents were miserable. On the flipside, however, there are those who do not mind flying in the teeth of strong opposition and even enduring the hardships of abject poverty as long as they are with the one they love.

Myo attempts to alleviate the sudden melancholy that casts a pall over their table, 'I would like to narrate an anecdote from my own experience if you can spare me a few minutes of your time, my friends.' He adopts the comically pompous air of someone at an important board meeting to tease them out of their sombre mood and they willingly turn their focus on him.

* * *

He scratches his head and dithers for a bit before he begins his story, because he does not really know how to begin.

'It is not easy to plan a wedding reception successfully,' he begins hesitantly. 'Nasty remarks and criticism are only to be expected from every corner. In my case, I needed to prepare at least six months ahead.'

Someone interrupts him, 'If we kept it simple, would we need so much time?'

Somebody else counters with, 'Man, it is a once-in-a-lifetime event for the couple. The bride would naturally want it to be grand and memorable for the bridal couple as well as their parents and relatives.'

Another friend chips in with his two pennies' worth, 'I will keep my wedding very simple and hold the reception at a monastery. This will not only help keep my costs down and provide a free lunch to the monks, I will also earn brownie points for a good deed. I think it will be an auspicious start for our wedding and our married life together.'

Another says, 'I would prefer a modern wedding held on the shore of a lake. It will be incredibly romantic like those we see in the West.'

A music enthusiast says, 'I will invite a band with great vocalists to perform at my wedding.'

Thus, each of them go on to describe their ideal wedding and Myo sits back and listens to the conversational ball he has set rolling.

* * *

Being inundated by so many excellent suggestions from close friends only makes things more confusing and the would-be bridegroom sighs gustily in frustration. It makes the task all the more complicated for him to make a proper decision. A determined, albeit resilient, mind is an absolute must.

The betrothed couple should decide their wedding without interference or advice from others.

The bride-to-be could make several demands on her betrothed—an expensive, pre-wedding photoshoot perhaps?

* * *

The venue, the menu, and the music for the wedding and wedding reception would have to be arranged. All this would be included in the guy's formidable to-do list.

It would be nothing short of a nightmare for the poor bridegroom before the wedding eventually takes place. He would have to endure many a sleepless night, burning the candle at both ends trying to arrange for cash flow for the expenditure he would inevitably incur. There could even be times when he would want to run away from the impending debacle; only his overwhelming love for his woman would keep him tethered.

He would often mentally review his diminishing bank balance. The remorseless ka-ching of the voracious marriage machine would incessantly resonate in his ears.

Being a hopeless romantic, he would unflinchingly shoulder the staggering expenditure, put it down to his burden of love and light-heartedly project his capability and reliability as a bridegroom.

There would be smiling faces all around and the sweetest of them would be his beautiful bride. One could go so far as to say that this is purely a labour of love.

* * *

What else? There is still so much to do. Take, for example, the bridal gowns and finery. If he places orders in advance for these things, it will cost less, although they will not be as perfect as the ones they could hire from the clothing rental outlets—where they could pick and choose their styles and colours from the wide ranges of yellows, pinks, and reds.

Speaking of which, if the bride wants the auspicious yellow as their wedding's theme colour and the bridegroom prefers pale white, it could lead to an unfortunate falling out between the couple. The groom will invariably yield to his lady's choices just so they did not break up over this paltry issue. Myo knows of several such cases.

And then, there is the choice of make-up artist—au courant these days. Needless to say, they come with a hefty price tag—up to two lakhs for one event. The bridegroom's opinion counts for nought in these matters. All he needs to do is nod unhesitatingly if he doesn't want to incur the wrath of his bride-to-be.

At this point in time, he can only look on helplessly as the bank notes merrily leap out of his pockets and vanish into thin air.

* * *

Another imperative is a good photographer and videographer who would record the whole ceremony. It is better to hire a proficient and well-known photographer for the event rather than an amateur. The pictures have to be perfect because the relatives on both sides would want copies of the photographs after the ceremony.

* * *

A good music band is another must-have. The fees for these bands vary and one would need to be ready to disburse at least seven lakhs for good music. Famous singers will need to be roped in for the event to satisfy the relatives just so the bridegroom is not put to the blush as being niggardly. The guests will appreciate the chance to be photographed with celebrities just so they can boast to their neighbours.

Last, but not least, will be an efficient and reputable master of ceremonies for the event. The MC's announcements about the bride and bridegroom have to be sweet and short otherwise the guests will grow impatient. This can cost almost half a lakh, although the rates change every year.

* * *

After that, he will just wait with bated breath for D-day. He will lead his bride by the hand into the sparkling hall and all their guests will admire the radiant couple. As soon as the MC is done with his introductions, the guests will take over with the mic and gush with accolades for the lovely bridal couple. This is the natural order of things at every reception.

The happy couple smile at everybody. The bridegroom feeds a spoonful of ice cream to his blushing bride. Everyone is happy, especially the parents of the bridal couple. The mother of the bride sheds tears of joy for having successfully carried out her maternal duties.

* * *

There are both good and bad things about planning a wedding. Frustrations, squabbles, and arguments are inevitable and they will be followed by concord. It happens all the time in the furore of the run up to the wedding. After this, the bridegroom will relax for a while and enter married life.

* * *

And then, *what will he expect?* According to an old Myanmar saying: A tattoo, building a pagoda, and marriage—these three things are very hard to undo.

Planning a wedding is neither as painful as banging one's head against a brick wall nor as difficult as belling a cat; but it is not as easy as whistling a tune either and it is certainly not a piece of cake.

It has to be rhythmic at every stage to produce harmonious jazz music and not a jarringly irregular drumbeat blaring out of a loudspeaker. That is all one needs to understand about planning a wedding.

Pluviophile

Adult Zaw Zaw wonders how he should start his story. His mind glitches, and he needs a few moments to organize his train of thought. Then, in a eureka moment, he hoorays in exultation, making him the cynosure of curious stares. The people at the bus stop probably assume he has lost his marbles. Seeing their bewilderment, he chuckles sheepishly.

From time to time, they anxiously crane their necks and peer down the road in the hope of catching sight of an arriving bus.

He had only just left the office. One of his colleagues had offered to accompany him part of the way home, but then changed his mind at the last minute, so Zaw Zaw arrived at the bus stop alone. As he sits down, he looks up and sees a clear, blue sky. It does not look like it will rain. Birds are flying in the sky and some circle over the pedestrian bridge.

* * *

When the rain buckets down unexpectedly, Zaw Zaw moves to the sheltered bench in the bus stop. If the bus is running late, he would have to spend quite a while waiting here.

With a sidelong glance he notices a couple seated beside him. Oblivious to the other people in the vicinity, they huddle together, hands clasped, to avoid the driving rain. They seem ensconced in their own cosy and romantic world.

People seeking shelter from the downpour hurry into the bus stop. Zaw Zaw plugs in his headphones and chooses a song he likes to kill his boredom.

* * *

A popular saying describes it perfectly: the rain of Yangon is just as hard to predict as the girls of Yangon.

The shining raindrops, splashing down merrily from the sky, invoke memories of his carefree childhood. A vivid scene appears in his mind's eye of himself as a child, splashing around in the rain.

His friends from the neighbourhood holler, 'Hey, Zaw Zaw! Come out and play football with us. Do not dawdle, man. We don't want to hang around here all day, waiting for you. Everybody is here.'

Zaw Zaw's mother, who has been busy making dinner, emerges from the kitchen to see what the hullabaloo is all about. Peeping through the doorway, she sees a playful group of boys at their gate. One lad is holding a plastic ball.

Her son, Zaw Zaw, looks up eagerly at her, 'Mom, please, let me go and play with them. I will be back soon.'

His mother agrees. 'But, Zaw Zaw, just be careful, okay? Your father will blame me if you accidentally hurt yourself. You know how brusque your father can get.'

Zaw Zaw is overjoyed. He hurriedly changes into a pair of shorts and races out.

'Yay, Zaw Zaw is in. I will take him on my side,' one of his friends shouts exultantly.

Another friend protests, 'No way! I already told you that he is on my side. You have your men. I have mine. Don't be so mean, Aung Aung.'

Zaw Zaw quickly steps into the fray, 'Let us flip a coin to decide.'

'Who wants heads? Who wants tails?' asks Aung Aung, 'Tails.'

The coin is flipped. When it hits the ground, it lies with heads on top. So, Aung Aung's side takes Zaw Zaw. The boys head to the large playground in their neighbourhood. They see some grown-ups already there, playing football. The boys choose another area of the playground.

They divide into teams. Just as they get ready to kick off, the rain comes pelting down. Nevertheless, the game starts.

All the boys race towards the ball. They collide into each other and tackle each other in the scuffle to get the ball. The boy who ultimately gets the ball passes it to Zaw Zaw who, in turn, deftly dodges and weaves past his opponents. He directs the ball towards the goal and kicks it hard.

However, the goalkeeper successfully intercepts the ball. Zaw Zaw, in frustration, vows to score the next time round. The goalkeeper sends the ball flying over the centre line and the boys, exhilarated and happy, set off again in pursuit.

When Zaw Zaw gets the ball this time, he dribbles the ball into the goal-scoring area and kicks it hard. The ball slams into the back of the net and he successfully scores a goal. His team cheers loudly, 'Goal! Goal! Goal!'

What an amazing feeling to score a goal!

They play hard and Zaw Zaw plays really well. He is called a 'striker' because his buddies are aware that he not only knows some clever football manoeuvres, he is an excellent goal scorer. Together, with his friends in their neighbourhood, he plays football in the muddy playground and loses all track of time.

They are wholly immersed in their game. Sometimes they erupt into arguments about scoring a goal and Zaw Zaw has to intervene and arbitrate because if their parents were to find out about the lads brawling in the rain, they would no longer grant them permission to play.

Zaw Zaw tells the combatants to shake hands and apologize to each other. Thus, the case is settled and they cheerfully resume play. Until the rain lets up, they continue to happily enjoy their game.

And then, their worried parents arrive at the scene, canes in hand, to stop their fun. If the adults had not appeared, the boys would have continued playing the game, which had become tantamount to a tour de force.

Some of the parents holler, 'Hey, you rascals! Come home immediately. You do know that you're playing on the bare, wet ground; you could be struck by a bolt of lightning.'

The boys are so intent on their game that they ignore the furious adults and carry on playing.

When Zaw Zaw gets home, he is muddy from head to foot, so his mom insists that he gets cleaned up before he sits down for dinner.

'Don't play out in the open so much, my dear. You could catch your death of cold and a fever if you get drenched in the rain; and then, what will I tell your father when he comes home? He will scold me for allowing you to go out when the weather is bad.'

Zaw Zaw understands his mother's concern because he is his parents' only offspring.

His father works all day in the office and usually brings home delicious treats in the evening. Sometimes fried noodles, sometimes fried rice. Zaw Zaw prefers fried noodles.

At the thought of noodles, Zaw Zaw remembers his appalling incompetence at using chopsticks. He could never hold the chopsticks properly and the cluster of noodles would invariably slither back into his plate. His father suggested that he should roll up the noodles on a fork and then nibble it off the tines. Those were happy times, indeed, whenever his father visited the Chinese restaurant on his way home from work.

At the dining table, knowing how much Zaw Zaw loved fried noodles, his father, who did the serving, lovingly piled on more noodles on Zaw Zaw's plate than on his own. Zaw Zaw loves his father so much because of his caring behaviour.

* * *

Zaw Zaw flinches at his mother's mention of his father's irascible temper. There were occasions when his father had lost his rag and caned his son.

'Please, Mom,' Zaw Zaw pleads, 'don't tell Father that I played in the rain today. Please keep it a secret.'

One day, Zaw Zaw caught a severe cold after playing in the rain. When his father came home, he berated his wife for her carelessness. She bowed her head and accepted the reprimand in silence. Zaw Zaw wanted to console his mom because she was paying the price for Zaw Zaw's foolishness.

During that time, his favourite snack was coffee and Myanmar pancakes—the aroma of which made his mouth water. He was famished after playing hard and he devoured them as his mom watched him affectionately, love surging up in her heart. He glanced at his mom, chomping hungrily until all the pancakes were gone.

He was a playful little lad, always keen to rush out and play football with his boisterous peers whenever it rained. Their yelling and shrieking reverberated through their otherwise quiet neighbourhood.

'Yay!'

'Goal!'

Their cacophony put the clamour of Mother Nature's gale force winds in the shade. This part of his memory remains trapped in his nostalgic mind. He also remembers some lively lyrics sung in the rainy season. They went something like this:

> When the rains come down, we'll take a shower in the rainwater,
> When Mom comes, we'll suck Mom's *beeboos*,
> When Dad comes, we'll break a coconut and eat it.

These lines are sung very merrily during the monsoons and every child knows the lyrics by heart.

They also know that everybody needs to watch out whenever they pass beneath the coconut palms during thunderstorms because, when the wind blows hard, the coconuts are liable to fall onto the heads of unsuspecting passers-by—it is a common occurrence in this neighbourhood.

The good thing about the rainy season is that the youngsters have an opportunity to snuggle up in bed and catch up on reading their comic books—the ultimate luxury in life.

* * *

Zaw Zaw is seated on a bench at the bus stop as the rain gains momentum and blurs everything. People hurry to get under the protective roof of the bus stop. He smiles to see the young couple, who share his bench, embrace passionately as the rain pelts down even more fiercely. He quickly suppresses the smile because he does not want people to mistake him for a perverted voyeur.

Sometimes, he misses something for no reason at all. It could be because the weather triggers nostalgia. As an adult, he loves to walk in the rain because he considers it a perk of being a grown up because he can make his own decisions without someone constantly chiding him for getting soaked in the rain. He enjoys walking in a heavy downpour just as much as he enjoys a drizzle.

He remembers his girlfriend holding his arm as he held an umbrella aloft; they enjoyed feeling the refreshing raindrops on their faces. They would walk for miles together to their neighbourhood. Then, they would part.

* * *

There is still no sign of the tardy bus and more and more people converge under the awning of the bus stop to avoid getting soaked. Zaw Zaw is still lost in his reverie.

Unlike these people, he loves the rain. Zaw Zaw looks at his sodden umbrella beside him. He pities it for some strange reason. He slips it into his bag and steps out into the wet street. There is still no sign of the rain letting up. Happily, he saunters down the road, revelling in the wonderful sensation of the rain falling on him. He is ecstatic.

Then, a word pops into his head: pluviophile. That word describes him perfectly.

Three Days at Inya Lake Hotel

It goes without saying, February's heat is as blisteringly hot as the summer. Who would want to endure such scorching weather? It induces profuse sweating with no respite from the sultry conditions.

To make matters worse, there are interminable traffic jams. The very thought of venturing out from downtown gives one the heebie-jeebies. Everything grinds to a standstill and I have no choice but to wait until the lane moves again. The stream of the cars crawls at a painfully slow pace in the public roads.

I am on my way to the Inya Lake Hotel, a structure built during the socialist regime, for the very first literary festival to be held there. The Irrawaddy Literary Festival will showcase both international and local writers and I look forward to participating in it.

I hail a cab near the Sule Pagoda and the taxi driver seems to know of the event. On the way, we are held up for almost ten minutes at the Bahan junction and then there is yet another traffic jam near Pearl Condo. After that, the cab

progresses easily along Kabaraye Pagoda Road, turning left
into the lane leading to the hotel.

I get off at the porch and walk towards the crowd standing
at the entrance. I scan the group for my senior writer, Sayar
Lay Ko Tin, who invited me to this event. People are at the
display cases, browsing through the books for sale, selecting
and buying books that pique their interest. I decide to come
back later and look at the selection of books, after I've met
with my senior writer.

Suddenly, I spot Sayar in the crowd and he waves me
over. He looks spiffy in his white shirt.

'Good morning. Here is your ID card for the festival.' I
see my name printed on the card that he proffers. I thank him.

'Let's go in,' he suggests. We walk through the lobby and
emerge through a door on to a terrace where several tables
have been laid. We sit at a table to discuss the topic we are to
present at the panel: Translation. Our session is scheduled for
11.30 a.m., after the poetry symposium.

After our chat, Sayar suggests we attend the first
session—the fascinating poetry reading, followed by
interesting discussions. It will give us an opportunity to meet
well-known poets. Towards the end of the poetry session, we
can slip out and head for Ruby Room A, where we will hold
our session.

Just then, a foreigner comes over and asks, 'Is it all right
to call out "psk . . . psk . . . psk . . ." to the taxi driver, or is it
considered rude?'

Imagine my delight to see that it is none other than the
famous author, Vikram Seth, standing in front of me. He is the
very person whom I longed to meet at this festival. *What luck!*

'It is okay, I guess,' I reply readily.

He seems to like my answer and smiles. I confess to him that I recognized him from his pictures on Facebook. He is quite a friendly person.

Another pleasant surprise is that the famous writer Yang Chen is with him. She is such a graceful lady. She stands beside him, looking fabulous in her pink blouse. I greet her cordially, '*Minglarpar* (auspiciousness to you)'. She is just as friendly as Vikram Seth.

They notice our ID cards and discover that we are writers from Myanmar. While we are chatting, there is an announcement that the opening ceremony is about to begin on the Sunset Terrace. We excuse ourselves and hurry to the place.

The venue is an open area overlooking the water. By the time we get there, the welcome address of the festival's organizer is already underway. After his speech, Myanmar writer Pe Myint helps inaugurate the event. The audience applauds. The festival has officially begun.

* * *

Then, we enter the ballroom where the poetry panel discussion is to be held. It is a spacious hall with spectacular chandeliers suspended from its ceiling. The auditorium is filled to the rafters with people eagerly waiting to listen to the discussion.

On the stage are the four panellists for the discussion— editor, James Byrnes; the translator, Ko Ko Thet; the moderator, Zeyar Lin; and the Pilipino poet. They begin the discussion by talking about the nature of their poems and analyse the poetry book *Bones will Crow*, which they had published.

* * *

Thirty minutes fly by. Sayar gestures to me that it is time to leave by tapping on his watch dial. We quickly walk upstairs.

Ruby Room A is mostly empty at first, but gradually fills up as people troop in, find their seats, and settle down.

We take our places in front of the audience and instruct the IT assistant to project our topic's title 'Translation and Adaptation' onto the screen.

Just then, two of my friends telephone to say they have arrived and are waiting in the lobby. Obviously, I cannot go to receive them, so I quickly whisper the directions to Ruby Room A on the phone, asking them to make their way to us.

A few minutes later, our session starts. Sayar is the first to stand up, providing brief introductions for each of us to the audience. Following that, the Myanmar writer, Thet Oo Zin, initiates the discussion and the subsequent talks, all of which proceed smoothly.

I am the last to speak and talk about self-translation because I know that even the world-renowned writer Rabindranath Tagore self-translated his works into English. My focus is on self-translation because, like him, I too self-translate my works into English.

The renowned Myanmar historian, a staunch supporter of my views on self-translation, is present in the audience. We discuss a few controversial usages of Myanmar personal pronouns, particularly *thu* (he) and *thu-ma* (she). Some writers advocate the use of the gender-neutral pronoun, thu, in the Myanmar language, asserting that there is no place for thu-ma in our mother tongue.

* * *

The festival exudes an exclusively literary ambience, effectively showcasing budding creativity in the field of literature. The backdrop of Innya Lake emphasizes its secluded and rarefied atmosphere. With no stirring of the February breeze, the light feels brighter than the usual January sunshine, making everything appear more vivid. Seated on the lawn of the café and sipping refreshing iced tea is exhilarating. Later, we indulge in aromatic green tea with friends—sheer luxury. The walkway along the lake is flanked by palm trees, which sway gracefully in the breeze. There is a quaint, wooden bridge at the edge of the water, overlooking the Innya Lake. It is the ideal spot for writing or drawing.

The Second Day

As our panel is not included in the programme for the second day, I have the leisure to explore the literary events. I wander from room to room to attend the various discussions, thoroughly enjoying myself.

As usual, I arrive at the hotel before the festival starts and hang around for a while in the lobby, wondering whether I should buy Vikram Seth's novel *Two Lives*. The previous day, during the post-lunch break, Sayar Lay Ko Tin and I had run into him again when he had unexpectedly come out onto the Sunset Terrace. He readily complied when we asked his permission to take a photograph with him. It was a rare opportunity indeed to have been able to meet him in person.

At the bookstall, I discover that I have very little cash in my wallet. However, I do want Seth's autograph, which means I need to buy the book. I am, therefore, in a dilemma about buying the book. As fate would have it, a lady comes to the shelf just then, picks up the book and buys it. I shrug and decide to buy it later. I continue to browse through the other books displayed on the stand.

When I eventually return to the bookstall in the afternoon, to my surprise, I cannot find any of Seth's books. When I ask the salesperson at the stall, she says that they are all sold out. I leave the Memorial Books stall empty-handed and disappointed.

* * *

I see foreigners loitering here and there. They seem to outnumber the local people at the festival and appear really keen about literature. Some are even enjoying the Myanmar puppet show. I can hear Myanmar's classical harp music playing somewhere in the background. The melody bestows auspiciousness into the surroundings. There are people seated on the lawns with friends and children. They look carefree and relaxed. It is probably the literary effect on everyone. Whenever races or nationalities differ, they converge in literature.

* * *

I hurry in to attend the panel discussion of Yang Chan and sit down just as it starts. In the audience, I see both young and old people. I notice a pretty, young Japanese girl trying to take the best photographs of the discussion from different angles. She walks audaciously down the main aisle to photograph the speaker. I appreciate her typically Asian decorum and modesty. She seems oblivious of my admiration.

The Third Day

The panel discussion by Vikram Seth, scheduled to start at 4.30 in the evening, is the last session of the final day of the festival. I feel that it is imperative for me to attend it because I have a genuine question to ask him.

I return to the hotel in the afternoon, hoping to meet Sayar Lay Ko Tin, who is also interested in Seth's discussion. When I telephone him, he is busy chatting with Myanmar's famous female author, Juu. So, I tell him I would wait for him outside the ballroom.

When Seth's discussion starts, I jot down some of the salient points from his talk. The moderator discusses the nature of his fiction with him. He is a prolific writer with books that are nearly 1,500 pages long. As far as I am aware, he has written more than six books and had probably made his debut with *A Suitable Boy*.

When I met him the previous day, he asked me if I had ever read his books. I had to confess that I had only read some of his poems on poemhunter.com.

Just then, Mrs Chan had interrupted to mention that she had heard that her book, *The Wild Swans*, had been translated into Myanmar. I told her that indeed, her book had been translated and was available at local bookshops. Unfortunately, its translator passed away a few years ago.

After his talk, Vikram Seth opens the floor to questions and several people in the audience raise their hands, so I have to wait for my turn. He responds to the questions from the audience first, quickly making notes and answering them as he goes along because the discussion is to wind up soon.

To my question, 'Do you have any suggestions for future writers?' he merely says, 'Live and write.' I thank him for his inspiring reply.

The end of his discussion signals the finale of the festival held on the Sunset Terrace. I walk out along with other people to attend the closing ceremony. It begins with the closing speech of the festival's organizer.

It is around 6.30 p.m. and the orange rays of the setting sun are reflected radiantly by the windowpanes. It is like the glorious swansong before the darkness silently drops the curtain on the festival.

Walking through the lobby, I can hear the jazz quartet playing some lively tunes at the bar. The music lingers with me as I exit the hotel alone.

I turn around for a final glimpse of the hotel and then stroll down the driveway to the gates. My steps are slow because I cannot help reflecting on the experience I gained from this festival.

To me, the name 'Irrawaddy' will always be synonymous with the words, 'Live and write, live and write.'

I take a deep breath and brace myself to look forward to the future. It will unfold exactly as I wish, or not. In that moment, I realize I had matured in literature.

10

An Urbanite Who Was in Love with Night

I adore night, I really do; although it does not mean I dislike day. I love night because of its serene silence and maturity. It is not as hyper as day. However, they are both a part of Nature—two sides of the same coin.

During the daytime, day carries out its duties diligently. One can even say that day is as busy as a bee; no time for laziness. It would be wrong to consider daylight a chore if one wants to progress. Day is the time to try harder and advance. This is the natural order of things. Day is for daily necessities: for earning, for studying, for life improvement, for family, all of those things; there is no rest in day, one has to work.

The guarantee for life will be lost if one were to slack off and relax during the day. The penalty will be remorse and regret if one fails to use the opportunities afforded by day; one can even end up envying another's success. Therefore, it is necessary to not squander precious daylight by falling asleep.

Incessant working during the day will ensure good results for both the present and the future. One needs to go to school during the day and study one's lessons properly in class, without daydreaming, in order to stay abreast with the times.

If one does not try as hard as the others, one will inevitably remain a follower rather than blossom into a leader. Also, one should never lose track of time because it is said that this is the age of education. Therefore, if life were a lifelong education, one should try to not take any rest, so that one can accumulate as much knowledge as is possible. One should make the effort to use the available time properly, otherwise one can be left behind and become envious of other people's success.

If someone wants to progress in life, it does not pay to trivialize one's time with wasteful pursuits or by falling asleep willy-nilly. One needs to be fully alert for potential opportunities and challenges. This is one of the prescribed texts for daytime. So, day is active, hyper, and dynamic like the rapids in a stream. This is its true elegance and can't be swapped for anything.

Now, I would like to talk about night.

True, I love night. But that doesn't mean I slack off during the day. I would like to reiterate, I work during the day without any breaks. That is the only way to make my life progressive and successful. It helps me create a beautiful life. Isn't this right? Therefore, I need to slog during the day.

Night is not like that. Look at everything that describes night—silence; quiet; serenity. Nothing like the hubbub of day.

* * *

Let me bring you to a tranquil night scene. Look at downtown pedestrians. They look relaxed. Some walk alone. Slowly. Leisurely. Some as couples. Arms linked. Gazing here and there. Easy. They take their time to examine the fabric before selecting it. No worries at all. Spending time and relaxing in the night-time.

Some head towards Mahabandoola Park (formerly known as Fytche Square in colonial times) for a stroll. Or go down to Strand Road to watch the sunset. Or go to Chinatown to taste the various culinary delights.

Is this applicable only to live beings?

No. Inanimate things are the same. Cars are parked quietly beneath the neon streetlamps like they are resting up for the next day's hectic activities. At this time, my favourite things to do are to order a cup of tea in a tea shop and lose myself in the music of Myanmar vocalists on the stereo. I can enjoy them comfortably. *Yes*. This time is for relaxation. I have to relax. Time to relax. Relax. Time to work. Work.

Thus, night and day are distinct realms. It is tasteful and worthwhile to take a stroll to the Strand to breathe in the breeze in the quiet flow of the moonlit Yangon River. The gentle breeze across the river soothes and pacifies the urbanites. I feel the same pleasant sensation as I saunter along the Strand in the moonlight. I do that to escape the suffocation of the congested, urban city. I never grow tired of inhaling the night air to alleviate my fatigue.

By a stroke of luck, I find an available seat near Pansodan Jetty and sit down on the bench to watch the gentle flow of Yangon River. As soon as I sit, my worries and fatigue vanish. I come here whenever I have the time. I look around and find some couples sitting on the buoy and others just enjoying the peaceful scenery. I see that a barge has already left the jetty for Dala's pier across the river. I normally see seagulls circling over the barge, but it is night-time now and they've all hidden.

Across the river lies Dala town, and people take a boat from Pansodan Jetty to get there. Some cross the coffee-coloured river for work in the city, while others get on the ferry for a day trip into town. From the decks of the boat they watch dozens of small sampan boats bob on the fast-flowing currents of the water.

I see smoke curl lazily from the chimney of the barge. My gaze lingers for several minutes and then I remember something. Quietly, I take out a piece of paper from my pocket. It is an essay written by one of my students. It is just a draft that I need to look at. The essay is about Yangon and Yangon River. It goes something like this:

> Dagon is the former name of Yangon City, which is situated along the Yangon River. Interestingly, this river is known by two names; it is sometimes referred to as the Yangon River and at other times as the Hlaing River.
>
> It is formed by the confluence of the Bago River to the east and the Myitmaka River in the north. The tidal range varies, depending on the sun and the moon. During Spring, its current is between four and six knots, with an increase in speed during the rainy season. The river flows from Yangon to the Gulf of Martaban in the Andaman Sea, which lies twenty-five miles to the southeast.
>
> Between 1786 and 1824, shipbuilding thrived along the riverfront due to the abundance of teak provided as building materials for ship hulls and masts. Over the forty-five-year period, more than a hundred large boats

and ships bound for Europe were constructed, totalling approximately 35,000 tonnes of building materials.

Most of these ships were sold in foreign ports, with some joining the East India Company's fleet. Upon completion of shipbuilding, mariners and ship owners were eager to depart from the Yangon River for other shores due to the presence of a wood-boring worm called 'teredo navalis' in the water. This worm was notorious for attacking the wooden bows of ships that remained in port for extended periods.

* * *

I feel that the essay contains valuable insights about the city and the river. I appreciate my student's efforts in composing such an essay. After reading it, I carefully fold the paper and tuck it into my pocket. Glancing around, I notice that the darkness has already settled on the horizon. In the parking spot along the embankment, a few cars are visible. As I gaze across the river, the city of Dala appears dim from this bank, silently bathed in moonlight.

Gazing upwards, I behold countless stars decorating the night sky. *What could possibly compare to the beauty of a night adorned so magnificently with stars?* It prompts contemplation. Thus, whenever I find myself in Pansodan Jetty, the idea of returning home becomes undesirable. This sentiment is one of the reasons I cherish night.

I truly mean it. Night is genuinely tranquil, devoid of hyperactivity. It exudes an elegant maturity, a serene beauty that can only be appreciated when experienced.

When I leave the jetty, I opt for a leisurely stroll along the carefree Anawratha Road to see the sparkling and dazzling shopping malls adorned with colourful bulbs, the radiant lights emanating from posh cafés, fashionable clothes displayed in store windows and exhibits that can captivate any craving of the soul. I firmly believe that these elements indeed crown the beauty of the night.

As I amble along, absorbing the sights, I feel incredibly soothed. With not many items on my to-do list, I walk casually, free from worries. Along the way I observe people and take in the surroundings. Upon arriving home, I look up at the sky; the moon is almost directly overhead. My desire to admire its beauty persists, preventing me from falling asleep. Eventually, I venture out to sit in the balcony and continue to gaze at the moon.

Thanks to the moon, the beauty of night is at its zenith. At this hour, almost everyone has retired to bed, save myself. I still crave the enjoyment it offers. That's precisely why I profess my love for the night.

I gaze at the moonlight embracing the roofs, roads, and trees—a silent splurge of light. Quiet. Elegant. They are the creations of the night and the moon. I savour the atmosphere, feeling a profound connection to the night.

Oh, Night! You are silent, quiet, and elegant.

Despite the distinct toll of the clock from Sule Fire Tower striking midnight, I resist the call of sleep. Now, it's twelve o'clock.

Realizing that day would follow night and night would follow day, I acknowledge the fleeting nature of nocturnal beauty. I cannot afford the indulgence of waking up late as my morning responsibilities await me. Tomorrow's class preparations and the return of the draft essay to my student cannot wait.

As much as I wish to fully embrace and savour my favourite night time, I have to content myself with this feeling, nothing more. Anything more will make me seem egotistic and not a true lover of beauty. Or so I ponder.

11

When You Talk about
What You Feel

Moe found himself at a loss, unsure of how to occupy his time as he settled into his chair. His mind drifted like an untethered kite, floating freely in the wind. Over the past couple of days, a weight, intangible but potent, had drained his strength, leaving him feeling listless. The ennui gradually took root in his mind and formed a mental barrier, making it impossible for him to focus on his job. Determined to address the issue, he resolved to confront it head on.

It was an abstract feeling and although he felt it, he couldn't quite put a finger on the sensation. Spontaneously, he picked up the pen from the rectangular lacquer pen holder on the desk in front of him. His intention had been to use his laptop, not the pen. Sighing at his state of mind, he looked at his watch—it was 4.15 p.m. He put his laptop away and stood up, grabbing his shoulder bag that lay aslant against the foot of the table.

Moe heard his inner voice say, 'Nostalgia is a state of mind inclined to reminiscing about someone or something cherished in the past. However, that person (or thing) remains absent, relegated to a certain period—whether it be brief, extensive, transient, or perpetual.'

Moe's best friend had passed away six months ago and he craved solitude while he grappled with his debilitating emotions of sadness and loss.

Being extroverts, both invariably hung out together, attending almost every party and soirée at the best hotels in the city. They were usually the last ones to leave a party. They breakfasted together at the local tea shops, sipping tea with savoury dumplings or mutton pastries, which crumbled as soon as one bit into them.

They shared such an excellent rapport that they were each other's confidantes. Whenever his friend was at a loose end, he'd telephone or text Moe and arrange to meet up at a café or a restaurant in one of the finest local hotels. He got bored during holidays, especially when their other friends went out of town.

People loved to reminisce about the town or village in which they were born and grew up, their schools, universities, and more, because places often served as landmarks to their lives. The locale invariably left its indelible mark on the inhabitants of the area.

A place frequented with one's best friend would become a repository of treasured memories after the friend departed. One, therefore, loved to return to the old haunts to dwell on the past and immerse oneself in the lonely sadness of nostalgia. You sat at the same table and ordered the same kind of coffee or listened to the same music to recapture the conversations you had shared to relive those moments.

* * *

The twenty-five-year age gap between Moe and his friend didn't impede their becoming fast friends. They had both had traumatic childhoods—with appalling fathers. Their heart-to-hearts on this subject helped heal their festering wounds.

Moe hadn't even heard of the local arthouse films until his dear friend introduced him to them. One day, his friend instructed him to meet him at their usual spot on the street corner at around 6 p.m. They hailed a cab and, on the way to the coffee shop, Moe's friend informed him that the plan was to watch an arthouse film—a genre entirely different from the usual Hollywood and Bollywood blockbusters that Moe usually watched.

There were not many people in the coffee shop that day—two girls and three boys were seated in the Mauve Lounge. When he stepped into the small room, Moe noticed it had been beautifully decorated with tinsel.

His buddy introduced him to the manager who happened to be an Englishman who could speak Burmese with distinct and perfect articulation. The manager welcomed them even as he was setting up the projector for movie show that night.

'Do you think we'll get a crowd tonight?' asked Moe's friend.

Brendan, the manager, turned his head to reply, 'I have already posted it on the shop's Facebook page.'

Moe's friend ordered a gin-and-tonic for himself and a cup of cappuccino for Moe. Choosing a table not very far from the projector, they noticed a young girl of about eighteen seated by herself. She may have been a singer because before her was a mic on a stand.

Moe and his friend struck up a conversation with her and discovered that she came all the way from Upper Burma to try to make her mark as a professional singer. On that day, she was in the coffee shop to be interviewed for the position of a crooner. She waited patiently while the manager completed fixing the projector before testing her voice.

Moe and his friend told her that they wrote for magazines and could arrange for her to be interviewed in the following month's issue if she was interested. She just smiled prettily and didn't say anything.

Just then, Brendan hollered, 'Okay, ready to roll. Let's watch the movie.' With that, he slipped a DVD into his laptop, which was already connected to the projector.

Both Moe and his friend enjoyed the film thoroughly and Moe resolved that he would come down to watch arthouse films even if his friend were away.

The movie they watched that night was about a Jewish lady who sought an official divorce from her husband. Every time she submitted her application to the divorce court, her husband would refuse to grant her the divorce. After several such disappointments over the course of eight or nine years, the woman descended into insanity . . .

After watching the movie, Moe felt that Myanmar women were very fortunate in their monogamous marriages. His friend, for whom traditional Myanmar marriage laws were new and seemed liberal, agreed wholeheartedly to his reasoning.

In accordance with customary Myanmar law, the betrothed couple had to have their wedding witnessed by seven neighbouring families around their home. If one's spouse were to stay away for six months from their partner, the marriage was considered annulled. Nevertheless, legal divorces were still carried out in a civic court by existing laws unless the case could be settled by the customary ones.

* * *

Moe planned to visit the coffee shop where he and his friend usually went to watch arthouse movies and enjoy excellent coffee, especially cappuccino. If he went there, Moe knew that he could imagine his best friend was beside him and reflect on the conversations they'd had there when he was alive.

Moe really needed to pull himself together. He couldn't spend the rest of his life mourning his dead friend. He still had a long journey ahead.

Moe was grateful to his friend for introducing him to the wonderful world of arthouse films and refining his taste in movies. He had fond memories of their wonderful time together.

Moe whispered to himself, 'Although you're no longer with me, you've left behind good memories that I will treasure for as long as I live.'

Moe stepped out onto the pavement and pedestrians hurried past him. Moe felt like he was in a void, invisible to those around him. He directed his footsteps towards the bus stand from where he would take a bus home.

Suddenly, and unconditionally, he was swamped by a bout of nostalgia . . .

Acting Contre-Coeur

At around 12.30, after lunch, Lwin was ready to leave his apartment. His lunch break was until 1.30 p.m. and an idea struck him . . . being a true-blue urban pilgrim, this was a golden opportunity to indulge in his favourite pastime: exploring the lesser-known places in downtown Yangon.

These days, the name Rebecca resounded in his head more than ever.

He was in a blue T-shirt and dark-blue jeans. He looked in the mirror as he slicked his hair back with coconut oil. Satisfied with his appearance, he headed towards Mahabandoola Road (formerly known as Dalhousie Road).

He turned left from Sule Pagoda Road and found City Hall on his left. Pedestrians walked past him briskly as he paused there to reflect on the history of the edifice. Painted in a beautiful shade of mauve, City Hall overlooked the central park in downtown Yangon, Mahabandoola Park. It was a triumph of Myanmar architectural design. Originally it

had been designated as the site for the secretariat, but that
had been moved to another location. City Hall now housed
the office of Yangon city's development committee.

In 1928, following a meeting to plan its construction,
the City Hall was designed by Myanmar architect Sithu U
Tin. It had played a crucial role in Myanmar's history. In
1884, the municipal office was moved from Shafraz Road to
Rippon Hall. The chairman of the municipal committee was
usually appointed by westerners but, in 1924, Dr Ba Yin was
appointed as chairman.

In the debate on the design of City Hall, U Ba Pe, a
prominent politician of the time, proposed constructing it in
the Myanmar style. He emerged victorious in the debate and
the contract was awarded to Sithu U Tin, who charged rupees
eighteen lakh and submitted his design.

Although they made an agreement to build it as
prescribed, finding the funds to ensure its construction could
commence in April of 1934 proved necessary. Eventually,
it was inaugurated on 15 June 1936. In the pre-colonial era,
Rippon Hall transformed into Town Hall, or City Hall.

Opting to modernize the city, Rangoon's area was
expanded, necessitating a much grander Town Hall.
Consequently, they invited contestants to contribute to the
architectural refurbishments and received thirty-six proposals.

Although the design by Mr Bray was selected, they found
that it was devoid of Myanmar craftsmanship. Therefore,
they awarded the construction contract to the Myanmar
architect, Sithu U Tin. Within an acreage of 7.28, the building
boasted four *pyatthats* (gradated turrets topped with small
umbrellas) and an Italian-style infrastructure. In a satirical
article, a newspaper likened it to the attire of the Myanmar

prince, Myin Gon Prince, who sported head gear combined with long pants.

To refurbish City Hall, architect U Tin had to closely examine ancient Bagan designs multiple times to assemble the motifs for the building. The front of City Hall faced Sule pagoda as a mark of reverence. The porch at the main entrance featured a dancing peacock at its centre.

It took four years to collate the building material for City Hall. The Myanmar arts expert Sayar Saing was roped in into the project.

On 13 July 1947, a Sunday, around 8 o'clock in the morning, a historic event took place at City Hall. The weather was fine with a clear, blue sky, and the people seemed excited and had gathered at City Hall where General Aung San would give a speech to the public. All the buses were suspended for that day. The chairman of the assembly was Thakin Nu, and the master of ceremonies was Thakin Tun Tin.

General Aung San stepped onto the podium, his hands behind his back in his usual stance, and delivered the boldest address in Myanmar's history. Some of his speeches faced criticism for their boldness as he pointed out the inherent weaknesses of Myanmar's citizens. According to General Aung San, these weaknesses arose from confusing freedom with self-indulgence, leading to the creation of public nuisances. It can be said that this was his last speech and it was one and a half hours long.

Among all the colonial buildings, City Hall stood tall and proud, showcasing pure Myanmar-style architecture to the awe of the visitors to Myanmar.

* * *

Lwin abruptly snapped out of his reverie when someone bumped into him. The man apologized and went on his way. Lwin realized that he needed to continue his walk towards the middle block of 36th Street to find the well named Rebecca.

A few blocks later, he turned left into a quiet neighbourhood with several parked cars flanking the street.

As he continued his stroll, he thought about the old city and its inhabitants. He remembered that there had been about two thousand Jewish people living in old Rangoon (that is former name of Yangon) and could find Jewish synagogues on the lower block of 28th Street.

The famous well was probably in this area. He had read about it in a feature article in the *Myanmar Times*:

> In olden days, in Rangoon (formerly known as Dagon), there was a well named after its donor, Rebecca. At that time, Yangon City had no water distribution system and people had to rely on wells, ponds and lakes in its vicinity.

Before finding the well, he unexpectedly ran into his friend, Aung, who also seemed to be out, taking a stroll in the bright afternoon sun.

'Hey, Lwin! Good afternoon,' his friend hailed him. 'Where are you off to? Don't you have some time to talk to me?'

Lwin nodded, smiling, 'Good afternoon, Aung. I didn't expect to meet you here. Where are you headed?'

'I've just posted some parcels to my brother who works in Singapore, and I'm returning from the post office in Yangon,' replied Aung with a shrug. Then he added, 'Sorry to hear about your break-up with Htwe. What happened? Did she not love you?' Aung looked at Lwin who looked nostalgic.

It was only then that Lwin was reminded of her. However, he didn't want to wear his heart on his sleeve and complain about his ex-girlfriend to a friend. Some things were better kept private.

Aung sensed Lwin's reluctance to share and didn't push him. In mutual, unspoken, concord, they both moved into the shade of a spreading *padauk* tree. Lwin decided to look for the well later. Pedestrians continued to surge past them as the two friends chatted in the middle of the pavement. They received some sour glances because they were a hindrance.

Just then, Lwin remembered someone who annoyed both him and Aung whenever they ran into him in the street or in a tea shop or at a bookstall. With an abrupt change in subject, Lwin said, 'This guy is a real nuisance. One day, I just couldn't bear it any longer and I yelled at him and told him to stay away from me.'

Aung looked blankly at Lwin, perplexed by Lwin's sudden change of topic. He couldn't, for the life of him, figure out who 'this guy' was. It clicked a moment later, and he realized that Lwin was talking about a pretentious bookish guy who bragged to everyone about having read all of Dickens' works during his teenage years.

Lwin continued, 'He rudely interrupted my conversation when I was happily chatting with one of my friends at the tea shop where we normally meet. It was near a bookshop and that friend of mine also knew him.'

Aung nodded.

'He boasted about his literary leanings and claimed the title of being the most learned guy on earth. Frankly speaking, neither my friend nor I had any interest in his ramblings. To make matters worse, he shamelessly bragged about having

landed a very lucrative job in a media company and told us
that his translations of movies were unrivalled,' Lwin broke
off his monologue to take a breath. Aung sensed that Lwin
was not done with his grouse.

'When a friend of mine, taking pity on this pathetic fellow,
nodded politely, I snapped and decided to rid ourselves of
this encroaching cockroach once and for all. I yelled, "Get
away from us, you moron!"'

Lwin knew that one shouldn't be unfeeling and rude
towards fellow human beings, but that guy went too far and
Lwin had been compelled to give him a piece of his mind.

* * *

All this time, buses were vrooming up and down the street,
drowning out Lwin's voice. Lwin raised his voice as he
continued his lament, 'You know, I agree that this guy does
have a certain talent, and I did try to support his zeal in learning
and accumulating knowledge. But look at what that ingrate did
to me—without my permission, he tried to get books on credit
from a bookseller who knew me personally. On account of our
relationship, the bookseller gave that lousy fellow the books
he asked for, but this shameless cretin never paid him back,
although he met my poor, gullible friend at his shop regularly.'

Aung remarked, 'Shameless maggot!'

Agreeing with Aung's remark, Lwin said, 'When I met
him at the tea shop the last time, he just butted in into the
conversation I was having with my friend. I told him that we
were talking about business and if he didn't understand our
discussion, he should wait until we were done. But this guy
didn't seem to understand what I meant.

'He continued to loiter around our table, repeatedly glancing at me and the plate of food before me. That made me lose my rag.

'I told him not to nag us because that would infuriate me. Only then did he shut up and back off. However, he had some cake and a cup of tea, and put it down on my tab. He has some nerve!'

Lwin tried to tone down his rancour, 'He was a distasteful and disgusting man, but I sometimes regret my harshness towards him. He exploited my sympathy, and now, I have become a villain in his eyes. I felt I had breached some social etiquette. If other people consider my response too harsh, they will definitely label me as a ruthless and merciless creature. I truly regret having ever met such a man.'

* * *

A bus honked several times at some people who were trying to cross the busy road. Lwin silently seethed at the bus driver.

'Oh, your experience was quite something, my friend, but, do go easy on that poor guy, okay?' said Aung.

Lwin nodded, 'Yes, I understand what you mean. I will try to be sensible next time.'

Out of the blue, that very same nuisance materialized beside them with a smug smirk on his face, akin to a tiger stalking its prey. As soon as Lwin noticed him approach, he turned his back on him and pretended to be absorbed in admiring the century-old colonial building. He was simultaneously devising a plan to get rid of the thick-skinned boor once and for all.

Reminiscence

A two-storeyed, brick house appeared before them. Thein, unable to believe his eyes, looked at Pay Thee, his childhood friend, in confusion.

'That's the house where you were born and grew up,' said Pay Thee.

Thein rubbed his eyes. It had been forty years since he had moved out to enjoy urban life in the city. His old home looked much changed compared to what it had been during the time he had lived here.

The house now seemed to be owned by a rich family. It had a spacious compound with high iron fences around it. It also had a portico where a modern car was parked.

Thein sighed and remarked, 'Oh, how things have changed. It all seems so different now.'

There were no more coconuts trees in front of the house. He remembered an unfortunate incident on one rainy day when a coconut dropped from a tree, causing a serious head injury to a passer-by. Ever since then, he avoided walking under the coconut trees.

After reminiscing for a while, he sighed, 'Where are all those coconut trees?' The subsequent owners probably cut them down when they tore down the old wooden shack and turned it into this brick structure.

Nevertheless, those sweet memories, indelibly imprinted in his memories, were hard to erase. 'It has been four decades, you know. I'm sure there aren't many of the old residents around here,' he remarked.

Pay Thee nodded, 'Yes, only two or three families still live here.'

'What about Maung Naing or Aung Zaw? Do you know where they are now?' Thein asked eagerly.

Pay Thee raked his fingers through his hair and shook his head regretfully, 'No, I don't know their whereabouts. I lost contact with them a long time ago. I am sure they are doing fine. As you know, Maung Naing's father owned a bookshop and Aung Zaw's father was a chef.'

Thein nodded thoughtfully, absorbing the information. After they left this area, they had settled in downtown where they ran a successful business by establishing a tea shop in a crowded part of the city. They were probably too busy with their daily routines to visit their old neighbourhoods or keep in touch with their old friends.

Thein sighed. He realized that the city in which he had been living had evolved over time and had changed irrevocably. The good memories lingered like artifacts permanently stored in the fabric of his mind. He no longer recognized his old neighbourhood because it had completely changed since his family had left this suburb.

* * *

Thein always remembered the joy of living in this house with his parents and sisters. Every evening had been enjoyable and exciting because they eagerly anticipated the blooming of the six o'clock flowers. It was such a pleasure to watch as the flowers bloomed before their very eyes and emitted their amazing fragrance.

He remembered his elder sister watching secretly from the veranda, wanting to slyly witness the flowers unfurl their petals. They had heard that the plant was very secretive and shy and would not bloom in the glare of public view.

They also knew that after the blooming, the moon would have risen high in the sky. They would watch it until their father returned home from work. Sometimes, he came home late, but there were occasions when he was early.

If he came back early, they could have dinner together as a family. Thein looked forward to those days because his father brought home treats like fried rice, fried noodles, and more. Sometimes, he even bought them toys.

* * *

Behind their house was a hill on which his school had been situated. He had attended the school since kindergarten, forming a few friendships along the way. There had been a girl whose name was too long to easily recall, making it a source of amusement for him and his classmates.

* * *

On some nights, when sleep eluded them, they would sit on a wooden bench in front of their house and his elder sister would regale them with ghost stories. While Thein liked listening to these tales, he was afraid of them and would huddle close to his sister for comfort.

'I assume you know that the old man who used to live at the end of this street passed away last week. People say he returns to visit his house at night. His family members don't dare to sleep and stay up late, keeping vigil. One of the household members claims to have seen the old man standing at the gate and waving. It's quite unsettling and I can't help feeling scared.'

She looked around at her young audience after saying this. In her mind, she felt pleased because her siblings seemed frightened—they threw furtive glances at the darkness behind them, wondering whether the ghost lurked there, ready to pounce on them and crack their necks.

His second sister piped up, 'Is that true, Ma Ma (sister)? I do believe you've made it all up.'

His elder sister countered, 'No, it's true. I heard about this from the victim himself this morning when I went grocery shopping.'

His second sister's eyes widened.

Suddenly they heard a clatter behind them and they all screamed in terror. Thein shrieked the loudest, 'Arr, *A-may-yay* (Mom)! *Tha-yal* (ghost). Tha-yal (ghost)!'

It turned out to be a cat jumping down from the tree onto the corrugated tin roof. When they saw the cat, their fear subsided.

Undeterred, his elder sister carried on, 'I will tell you another one. It was about a *peta*. Do you know the meaning of peta? It means "wandering ghost". They're voracious and hungry all the time. They become peta because when they were alive, they were avaricious. Their body is huge, with outsized ears and large eyes. Strangely enough, they have a very small mouth and so they can't eat properly, which is why they're hungry all the time.

'They sleep with their long ears wrapped around their body.' Thein's mind boggled as he tried to imagine the creature. Fear crept up his spine again, but his curiosity outweighed his terror, compelling him to listen to his sister's macabre tale.

He needed to pee urgently, but he controlled the urge because he did not want to miss out on a good ghost story.

Just then, they heard their mother calling to them, and the storyteller quickly stood up. She knew that if their mother found out about her spooking her younger siblings with ghost stories, she would get a beating.

* * *

Thein had a sister who was daredevil and incredibly agile at scaling the betelnut trees that surrounded their modest house. She was careful to ensure that she indulged in her adventurous exploits when their parents were away, conducting business downtown. In every competition involving climbing the betelnut tree, she emerged the winner.

Their house was a wooden, two-storeyed structure. For some obscure reason, Thein preferred the upstairs. One day, they were thrilled to find newborn mice in a drawer. They were tiny, pink things. The children did not tell their parents about their discovery.

All their neighbours were very friendly, except a family who lived immediately next door. They were pretentious braggarts, claiming to cook chicken when, in fact, they were frying watercress.

It was the proper etiquette in the locality for people to announce it when they fried or cooked strong-smelling food, to avoid upsetting old or ailing people in the neighbourhood who were allergic to such odours.

They loved to play in the large compound next door, where his sister befriended a girl of the same age. He remembered her greeting them cheerfully for Christmas.

Revolution Park was in their vicinity and, once a year, when Revolution Day came around, it was truly exhilarating to watch the fireworks display from their house's balcony.

He had so many great memories of that house. Now it was a brick building with other occupants. Back when they lived here, it used to be so much more down-to-earth and friendly—a place with good human relationships. But those days were long gone, replaced by other things.

Despite living in a new house, Thein yearned to return to his old house and reminisce about the good times he had had there. He was glad he had an opportunity to share with people how nice their old house was, although it appeared meagre and squalid.

Thein remembered their joy and laughter whenever they played games like *Htote See Toe* (a kind of outdoor game, mostly played by girls), *Nyaung Pin Tasay,* and *Shwe Swon Nyo* with the neighbourhood children. It had been a simpler and unsophisticated era and they hadn't known much about TV or computer games. Yet, it was a happy time as their games were well-suited for the children who played and had fun together.

Whenever they played Shwe Swon Nyo, Thein took the role of *Mi Htwe,* the youngest in the group. He was pampered and loved by everyone. In the game, he needed to hide behind a line of players while a person who assumed the role of Shwe Swon Nyo tried to catch him. It was great fun because he felt that he was protected by other players.

Their physiques developed well because of all the energetic outdoor games they played. Simultaneously, they understood the importance of unity and teamwork, skills that would be invaluable in their adult lives. Furthermore, their traditional games were preserved for posterity and passed down to the generations that followed.

His father invariably brought home good food and treats for the family whenever he returned from work, and they would all sit together and enjoy the meal. He believed that a house is a place where family values such as caring, loving, and sharing with each other were instilled.

* * *

Thein remembered the Chinese temple on the hillock across the street, where his uncle sometimes took them in the evenings. Inside the temple, he saw toy houses, model cars, and other items crafted from colourful paper suspended on a bamboo frame. He couldn't understand why they had been strung up on the frame.

His uncle later explained that these toys were intended for departed family members or relatives. Lighting them up symbolized the belief that these toys would appear in heaven with their loved ones.

It was great to see the origami models and Thein wanted to play with them although they were not meant to be played with.

* * *

Near their house was a restaurant called Burma Kitchen, which served as his father's watering hole where he drank alone or with his friends. His father took him there sometimes to buy him snacks like fried chicken wings, fried rice, etc.

* * *

In those days, ice cream cones were a rarity and could only be found in a place called *Dhar-hlee-yay-khal Chaung* where they needed to cut those creamy, frozen blocks into small thick cubes for the kids to enjoy. He liked them very much indeed.

* * *

They had been standing before the house for almost an hour. Eventually, Thein's childhood friend, Pay Thee, suggested that they go to the tea shop across the street and reminisce some more.

Thein nodded and cast a final glance at the house before turning to the tea shop.

Fame

Min and Tun stood at the corner of Pansodan Street and Merchant Road in downtown Yangon (known as Rangoon in colonial times), in front of a domed, three-storey building, which had been painted a light yellow.

Min started to explain about the building, intoning sonorously, 'This building was built around 1906 and is over a hundred years old. It belonged to two Jewish brothers who lived in Rangoon during the colonial times.'

'Jewish brothers? Really?' said Tun in disbelief.

Min nodded in affirmation and picked up the thread of his narrative, 'Look at the aesthetics of its façade and Italianate columns.'

The word 'aesthetics' sounded impressive to Tun who just scanned the entranceway as they were about to step in. He beheld the beautiful dome atop the building. The first thing to grab their attention upon setting foot inside were the seasoned tiles and an old wooden staircase.

Min noticed Tun's keen interest and said, 'You see these tiles, right? Do you have any idea where they originally came from?' Min had adopted the buoyant air of a trivia-quiz master.

Tun ruefully shook his head. He marvelled at the way two Jewish brothers had managed to procure such gorgeous tiles for their floor and assumed that they had probably been both rich and parsimonious. In one of the history books about the Jewish population in old Rangoon, Tun had read that there had been about two thousand Jews in Rangoon during the colonial times.

Today was just as boring as any other Sunday, and although the sky was clear and the weather balmy, they found themselves at a loose end, so they decided to take a tour of the city. Min chose the spot to begin their explorations—the Sofaer building.

The stunning building they had constructed had been named Sofaer's Building after the two Jewish brothers, Isaac and Mayer Sofaer. Tun was lost in admiration of their initiative in negotiating the sparse trade routes, which had been in existence at the time, to procure commodities from abroad to satisfy the needs of the residents who had settled in Rangoon.

Tun learned that a hundred years ago, these areas were exclusively for the Europeans, while the Chinese community had to make their homes far away from the downtown quarter—which later became known as Chinatown. A series of banks were established in Chinatown and to this day, they provide banking services to the public, although ownerships were changed after the nationalization process in 1962.

In the city where Min and Tun resided, although several buildings had been given proper names, Sofaer Building stood out among them all with its massive structure. Tun couldn't figure out where those tiles had come from and he asked Min. He replied that the tiles had come all the way from Manchester.

'These two Jewish brothers were educated at St Paul's School, which had been founded by French missionaries. The school is now known as BEHS No. 6, Botahtaung. In those days, this boarding school exclusively catered to the children who hailed from rich families. The famous alumni of the school included Spike Milligan and several others who held influential positions in the government offices,' Min explained. Tun and Min walked up the stairs to the first landing of the building and found a large window facing a building called Rander House.

In response to Tun's raised eyebrows, Min explained, 'Rander House was built by Gujarati merchants. In 1917, when the owner of Sofaer suffered financial difficulties, they lost this building along with all their other properties. The Indian Surti traders who owned Rander House across the street acquired this building.'

Tun noticed a *lawkanat* (a Myanmar figure of peace) sign above a doorway leading into the huge hall, the Lawkanat Art Gallery. Min followed Tun, who wanted to go into the gallery and see the exhibits.

'This art gallery was established in the 1970s and is one of the oldest galleries in Yangon. Its founding members were Myanmar artists such as Hla Shein, Kin Maung (Bank), and Paw Oo Thet. They established it with the aim of nurturing and supporting Myanmar's contemporary arts,' explained Min.

'Did you know we had a photo studio of Peter Klier, a German photographer who came to Burma in 1877, in this building?' asked Min. Tun felt that this building was replete with interesting stories. Amazing! This building was akin to a museum with a wealth of information. Tun was grateful to Min for having brought him here.

When they sat down on the wooden bench at the centre of the gallery, Min picked up his tale about the Jewish brothers, 'Meyer was apparently considered a business-minded person, while Isaac, a dreamer. They imported delicacies from around the world—sardines from Norway, olives from Spain, and whisky from the British Isles and sold them together with Vafiadis Egyptian cigarettes, Lighthouse Munich Beer, and candies imported from England.

'Another interesting thing is that they have a descendant (Isaac's son, Abraham) who became an actor later in his life.'

'Actor?' repeated Tun.

'Yes, actor.'

'Do you know which film he appeared in?' Tun asked, his interest piqued.

'After the death of Isaac Sofaer in Rangoon in 1926, most of his family moved to India. After WWI, Abraham left India to try his luck on the London stage. Later, he moved to Hollywood and appeared in the film *A Matter of Life and Death* and made a guest appearance in the first season of the television series *Star Trek*.'

'Oh, wow!' gasped Tun.

'The rest of the Sofaer family settled mostly in the UK and in California, USA,' Min concluded.

It felt like an anticlimactic ending to an illustrious family like the Sofaers. In any case, Sofaer's Building was a landmark in their history that continued to uphold the family name although they relinquished their claim to the building a long time ago.

Tun marvelled at the Sofaer family's spirit of adventure—coming all the way from the Middle East, following the trade routes charted by the East India Company and the British Empire; they came to the city, Rangoon, to establish a successful business empire that culminated in the construction of this beautiful edifice, exemplifying their prowess.

As Min and Tun left the building, they saw people walking down the street without bothering to even glance at the building. They chalked it up to either ignorance about the resplendent history of the building and its owners or their preoccupation with arriving at whatever their destination was as soon as possible.

Min asked Tun which place he would like to visit after the Sofaer Building.

Tun promptly replied, 'Pansodan Jetty.'

'Superb!' exclaimed Min.

Wrapping his arm around Tun's shoulders, Min led him down to the jetty and sought in his mind for another story to tell his friend.

Under his breath, Min softly recited the poem of Pablo Neruda who came to Burma around in 1927 to work in the Chilean Consulate in Rangoon. He invoked the poem for inspiration to narrate another story.

'I came late to Rangoon
Everything was already there:
A city of blood,
dreams and gold,
a river that descended from the cruel jungle into the
stifling city . . .'

Charm

It was depressing to see everything at a standstill in the city. The streets were empty and very few people were seen in the city streets running their routine errands. Moreover, the torpor only made things worse.

Even the old woman who sold fries from her shabby kiosk at the street corner seemed to lack her usual enthusiasm when a middle-aged man bought some of her fries. The very air was dull and motionless in the listless sunshine.

He wondered what calamity had befallen the city in which he lived and where the people of vitality had vanished. He looked around to see people lethargically carrying on with their humdrum activities.

There was a conspicuous lack of smiles in the sea of sombre and sullen faces. The pedestrians walked on, preoccupied with other things and seemed to have forgotten to glance around them. He sighed as he picked some fries from the vendor.

He selected a bag of chickpea fries, gourd fries, and a samosa and asked the woman to pack them for him. He counted out some money from his wallet and paid for the snacks.

'Please, also give me some tamarind sauce rather than chilli sauce,' he said.

The old woman mechanically put it into the paper bags.

Silently, he collected his change from the vendor and went home.

He lived on the second floor of a house that was located on the main road. He had to walk upstairs because the lift was broken.

He looked out at the street and saw cars and other vehicles. In his eyes, they seemed to lack their customary vim and vigour and were crawling along slowly. Although he shook his head, he couldn't rid himself of these peculiar notions.

He sighed.

He decided he needed to cheer up, so he left his apartment again and walked down to the convenience store, where he knew he could find the charming salesgirl. Just looking at her magically raised his spirits.

He couldn't quite put his finger on how or why she managed to dispel the gloom that settled on him from time to time. He lacked the word to describe the feeling or the potency of her charm.

He crossed the main road to get to the store. The glass doors at the store slid open automatically, triggered by the sensor. He spotted the salesgirl behind the counter, and she looked up at him when she sensed his presence. Her face, as always, bore a light expression. He glanced at her and then walked over to the refrigerator where the juices were displayed. He chose a juice box to have with his lunch.

As he paid for the juice, he looked at her again. Her innocent smile was unadorned and genuine. It felt good to just look at her. She was someone who could immediately restore his good mood. When he stepped out of the store, the wind whistled around him, and he felt like he was walking on air. Charm was contagious, knowing no boundaries. Could charm be nurtured, or was it intrinsic? Was it eternal or ephemeral?

* * *

He could not comprehend the myriad functions of the human mind, unfurling the various emotions: rage, happiness, wonder, and so on. He felt his weary mind needed solace at times, and even something as simple as admiring a sunset or gazing at the sky made his worries less weighty.

This story about charm began unexpectedly. One morning, at dawn, as he stood on his veranda, besieged by boredom at the mere thought of a long, humdrum day yawning before him, he noticed a girl who seemed blithe and carefree as she hauled open the heavy shutters of the convenience store across the street. He watched her, admiring her lithe movements and envied her cheerful light-heartedness.

Later, he discovered that she was a salesgirl at the convenience store. Subsequently, almost every morning, he positioned himself on the veranda to catch a glimpse of her. Like clockwork, she arrived at the shop at around 6.30 a.m. Her T-shirt was emblazoned with the emblem of the company that had opened the chain of convenience stores in the city, and she toted a haversack on her back.

It was impressive to observe the determination and skill with which she heaved open the heavy metal shutter, channelling all the strength in her slim, frail body. A few minutes after she had entered the shop, she emerged brandishing a broom and a scoop, to deal with the dirt that had accumulated overnight.

She dumped the rubbish into the trash bin on the pavement in front of the shop. Then, she hailed the vendor who sold boiled peas two shops down and placed an order for K200 worth of boiled peas for her simple breakfast.

A customer had already come into the store by this time. As soon as she had dealt with the customer, she returned to the boiled-peas vendor. And then she disappeared into the store for a while. At about 8.30 a.m. when the adjacent shop opened, she emerged from her store and went over to chat with the guy. It was probably an enjoyable conversation because she smiled all the while and was still smiling when she returned to the convenience store. This was her morning routine every day and it happened before my eyes.

* * *

Every morning, his lethargy evaporated and he perked just at the thought of watching the charming girl from his veranda. He began to appreciate the small pleasures in life like the melodious chirping of the sparrows on the padauk tree in front of his apartment and he began to find life interesting again. He wondered whether happiness was, in fact, a rush of adrenaline, although he wasn't sure. His conscience battled with unsettling thoughts.

He sensed his inappropriate fascination with the young girl and his strange obsession with spying on her every morning. He wasn't sure what had happened to him. He spent almost fifteen to twenty minutes covertly observing her before returning indoors to get ready for work.

In reality, he had succumbed to the enchantment of her charm—a timeless virtue of human existence. In his mind, he was young again. He knew that people sometimes wished to recapture their lost youth and innocence—they felt miserable to find their youthful vim, vigour, strength, and joie de vivre draining away.

* * *

He sighed softly as his mind grew sombre, and his happy-go-lucky mood evaporated temporarily.

He saw some somnolent pigeons perched on the façade of the tall building opposite his apartment, cooing listlessly. Just then, a swallow swooped around, its energy contrasting sharply with the lazy pigeons as it frolicked joyfully in the air.

As he watched it, his spirits lifted and prepared to go to work, resolving to start every new day with renewed strength and vigour.

Nyaung Hnin Noodle

The entire household was in a flurry of activity today, preparing for my sister's twentieth birthday. Mom had picked up her basket and gone shopping to the nearby market to buy meat and other groceries. She intended to showcase her culinary skills today and whip up delicious food and treats in the kitchen.

In the olden days, people celebrated their birthdays in the traditional Buddhist way by visiting a pagoda to donate candles and joss sticks to the image of Buddha. In addition, they paid homage to their parents, reflecting on the virtues their parents had bestowed on them.

In more recent times, birthday celebrations were very different. People typically ordered a cake from a popular bakery, lit candles on the cake and blew them out before cutting the cake. Everybody joined in a joyful rendition of the song 'Happy Birthday to You,' and the cake slices were then distributed to friends and family.

* * *

My parents preferred to follow the traditional way and cook family recipes handed down through generations on this special occasion. During yesterday evening's family meeting, I learned that my sister wished to invite five or six of her friends from school to spend the day with us at home. They would arrive around 9.30 a.m.

Our house was in downtown Yangon, just a few minutes away from the shopping centre Bogyoke Aung San Market (formerly known as Scott Market). Previously, most of the streets bore British names; however, they were later changed back to their original Myanmar names as people didn't appreciate the Anglicized names given to the streets in their neighbourhood.

* * *

Stirring the bubbling contents of a pot with her ladle, Grandma called out from the kitchen, 'Thinza dear, are you ready? Come and help me with the arrangements for your birthday.'

'In a minute, Grandma,' Thinza replied. 'Please ask Tun to lend you a hand for a bit now.'

I was in my room, engrossed in a book, but I overheard their conversation. Setting the book aside, I went into the living room where Mom was setting the table for our guests. Spotting me, she said, 'Tun, honey, lend Granny a hand in the kitchen: she's preparing Nyaung Hnin noodles.'

My mouth watered and my stomach rumbled at the mere mention of Nyaung Hnin. I didn't know that this was on the menu for my sister's birthday. I had assumed that we would order in chicken curry and parathas in honour of our guests. I guess they had changed the plan at the last minute.

I replied, 'Sure, Mom.'

The kitchen was redolent with the enticing aroma of the chicken curry and Granny was still diligently working on her noodles.

'Granny, are you nearly done?' I asked playfully. 'I'm famished.'

She smiled, tousling my hair, 'You naughty boy! You were supposed to help me, right? And now you want to eat it?'

She stirred the golden gravy in the pot with a wooden ladle. I saw bits of tender chicken and blanched onions in the simmering liquid. It smelled so tantalizing that I could no longer resist it and begged, 'Granny, please, please can I try some?'

Casting me a mock scowl, she scooped out a spoonful of the golden gravy and held it to my lips. I blew on it and tasted the delicious concoction. 'Ooh, it's yummy,' I exclaimed.

Granny beamed and said, 'It'll be ready in a few minutes.' With the captivating aroma of her dish lingering in the air, she stirred in some more ingredients into the gravy, which smelled even more wonderful.

As I wiped the cutlery and plates with a napkin, a thought occurred to me. Although we'd had these noodles quite often, not once had I asked Granny about the story of the noodles. Just then, my sister, Thinza, casually strolled into the kitchen.

'Tun, what are you doing here? You're supposed to be with Mom.'

'Mom asked me to help Granny, so here I am.'

Hearing my explanation, Thinza promptly vanished into the living room.

I turned my attention to the fascinating noodles, 'Granny, we've been enjoying this noodle dish for years, but I do not know anything about it. Do you know who created its recipe?'

Granny paused in her stirring. 'Why this sudden curiosity, Tun? I'm busy at the moment; I'll share the story with you later. Hand me that large bowl, my dear, so I can pour this gravy into it.'

Soon the bowl brimmed with Granny's rich gravy. She carefully unwrapped the parcels of flat noodles and arranged them on the tray. Meticulously, she organized an array of appetizers and condiments on the table.

There was an unwritten rule about serving these Nyaung Hnin noodles: we needed to use our fingers to transfer the noodles into our plates. This made it all the more delicious. What set these noodles apart was their distinctive golden-yellow hue, deviating from the usual white colour of noodles, and Granny told me one day that this was because the noodles had been smeared with saffron powder.

Granny told me to tell Mom when all the cooking was completed. By then, Mom had already laid out four circular tables in the living room. She told me to fetch the plates, serving dishes, and cutlery. Following her instructions, I laid five plates along with flatwares on each table. The cutlery was exclusively for our guests because we knew that some people felt awkward about eating with their fingers, although all of us in our family were used to it.

Before long, Thinza's friends arrived, one after another, bringing gifts for the birthday girl. They exchanged greetings and gave their gifts. Soon they were all seated at their respective tables, ready to celebrate the occasion.

They chatted incessantly with one another and seemed very happy. Thinza looked stunning in her pink blouse and her trendy hairdo. She busied herself ladling gravy into the plates on which the noodles had been served. She moved around from table to table. Everyone appreciated the dishes and asked for second helpings of the gravy and noodles.

I felt proud to have been able to treat our guests to the family recipe. That rekindled my curiosity about the origin of the noodles. Just then, Dad arrived with the lovely birthday cake. Thinza blew out the candles and everyone sang 'Happy Birthday to You'.

After cutting the cake and distributing the slices, the party wound up by 11 a.m. Thinza sought Mom and Dad's permission to go out with her friends to watch a newly released film at the local cinema. My parents agreed. Thinza and her friends thanked us and bid us goodbye before hurrying away to buy movie tickets.

I cleared the table and helped with the dishes. Granny sank into her comfortable easy chair in the veranda of our apartment. The veranda overlooked a large school compound that had beautiful, tall trees. It was quiet on this day because it was a holiday for the school.

I sat down by her side and massaged her limbs. She looked at me and smiled. Aware of my curiosity, she patted my head affectionately. With imploring eyes, I begged Granny to tell me about the history of noodles.

Raising the cup of green tea to her lips, she took a sip and cleared her throat before starting the story.

* * *

Nyaung Hnin lived in a small village in an island called Balukyun, which means Ogre Island. The word 'Nyaung' is derived from the Mon language and translates into 'Auntie'. In Myanmar culture, women, particularly for older women, are normally honoured with the title 'Daw'. The village's name was Tawkanar, a Mon word. There were over sixty villages in the island, primarily inhabited by Mon people.

They mostly grew paddy and some earned their livelihood by fishing because their island, surrounded as it was by the fast-flowing Thanlyin River that flowed into the Andaman Sea, lent itself to this trade. Nyaung Hninn was not only related to us, he was also my granny's neighbour and was five years older than she was. Before she started selling noodles in the village, she was a rice broker.

She often travelled to Mawlamyine, a port city across the island, to sell paddy. This was during the socialist regime and business in the port boomed, thriving with the influx of smuggled goods from Thailand that were very popular.

In the early nineteenth century, the British occupied Mawlamyine. George Orwell, a renowned British writer, then known as Eric Blair, had an aunt who lived in Mawlamyine. Even to this day, George Orwell's house in Mawlamyine is a great tourist attraction.

My grandmother's rice trade flourished until my grandfather died in a shipwreck. Out of frustration and despair, she stopped doing the trade and remained jobless until, one day, she found a recipe and created a kind of noodle. Even as a spinster, she had been very interested in cuisines and culinary arts. Mawlamyine women, or Mon women, were famous the world over for their amazing recipes.

One day, Nyaung Hnin remembered the recipe for a style of noodle curry she had enjoyed in Mawlamyine with her beloved husband. While recreating it, she incorporated some ingredients that would complement the dish. She stirred the curry until it started to thicken and began to resemble a normal noodle-curry dish.

Her modifications of the ingredients helped generate a brand new dish of her own, although she didn't realize it. She poured the gravy into the small bowl of flat noodles. She stirred in some pounded peas, added a teaspoonful of tamarind juice, and a pinch of chilli powder. She tasted it. It was delicious.

Then, she had a brainwave and decided to sell the noodle curry in the village as a snack, available at any time of the day. People would love it. She was delighted by her brainchild.

* * *

Granny paused and sipped her green tea before continuing, 'Many years later, when I asked her how it had been done, she taught me how to cook it. The people in the village loved her noodle curry and named the dish after her: Nyaung Hnin Noodle.

'She started selling it in the 1970s. It's nearly fifty years now. She passed away in the 1980s.'

I found this fascinating and tried to visualize Nyaung Hnin. She had probably been as thin as Granny, who was active and mindful in everything. Much like her grandmother, Granny loved to cook, and she had probably inherited her grandmother's desire to provide people with good food.

I realized that our family recipe had been passed down through generations and remained relatively unknown outside of our family and some village relatives. Even to this day, we still relish this noodle curry and make it whenever we can. I felt that chronicling this interesting snippet would be valuable for posterity.

A Mosaic of Life

Gingerly holding his debut book like it were a blue sapphire, Naing felt quite elated with his accomplishment. He thought about the amount of time he had spent to get here—over two decades. Phew! He remembered scribbling down his ambition to become an English author on the back flap of a textbook when he was a high-school student. That doodle at the back of his book was probably the proverbial writing on the wall for his journey into authordom.

He had been fortunate enough to attend private tuition, which had been arranged by his classmate, during the summer holidays. His classmate, Tin, had telephoned Naing to ask whether he would like to join a conversational-English class at his place. Naing readily agreed because Naing wanted to learn to speak English fluently and this opportunity was a godsend for him. Since then, he had developed a single-minded purpose in life to write a book and he often looked at the expressive line penned in his childhood to remind himself of his ambition.

Naing was the only person in his family who was passionate about learning English. His parents, being devoid of good schooling, laboured hard to support his education by running a grocery shop. Naing, left to his own devices, worked his way through difficulties in learning English. Nonetheless, he remained resolute about becoming articulate and well-versed in English as he grew up. His fluency alone would qualify him for a high government office; thereafter, he would interact with the literate and the elite.

Naing met his first English teacher, U Tun, at his friend's house, and he liked the way the teacher guided them through the intricacies of the English language. The teacher, Tun, used a textbook titled *Progressive English Course*. Even though Tun had graduated from Rangoon University just three or four years ago, he had been studying English with a well-known Rangoon University alumni couple who offered private tuition classes with minimal fees. Naing's respect for U Tun deepened when he discovered that U Tun had learned the rudiments of English in jail, where he had been detained for his involvement in the political activities of 1974.

After his release from prison, U Tun resumed his interrupted university course and graduated with a major in psychology. As was his habit, U Tun rose early every morning to revise his English. Aware of his teacher's unstinting efforts, Naing was inspired to do the same. U Tun was punctual, and he used an effective method to teach English. Following his guidance, Naing's English became flawless, and he enjoyed learning and refining it. His decision to be an English writer was further reinforced and secured.

* * *

Naing's train of thought was abruptly derailed when the publisher, U Myint, gently touched his shoulder and said, 'Ko Naing, I thought you would like the cover illustration and our presentation of the book.'

Naing smiled, nodded, and thanked U Myint for bringing out the best quality of his book for the public.

Publisher U Myint continued, 'Here are the rest of the royalties I owe you. How many complimentary copies do you want for your friends?'

Naing replied, 'Twenty copies should do.'

U Myint smiled at Naing's humility and agreed, 'All right. I'll take care of that right away.' The deal was as simple as that.

* * *

Soon Naing left the offices of the White Swan Publishing House and hurried home. On the way, he telephoned some of his friends and shared his success with them. There was a perceptible quiver of excitement in his voice. He invited them to come on Thursday morning to the tea shop where they usually hung out.

Impulsively, he stopped at a less-crowded place in the street and opened his precious book to the first page, and read the italicized dedication: *'Dedicated to those who taught me English, especially Sayar Tun.'*

His mind drifted to the past as a series of episodes popped up like fluttering of flashbacks.

* * *

'NO WAY! No, you cannot be a writer. If you become a writer, how can you make enough to make ends meet?'

Although Naing and his father didn't see eye to eye on this point, Naing dug his heels in. He knew of writers who lived fairly well; however, his father wholly rejected his arguments and insisted that Naing pursue a career in a more secure profession instead. Ever since then, Naing fell out with his father and they stopped speaking to each other.

Naing had suffered severe teenage angst because of his father's peremptory dismissal of his choice of career. At this impasse, he wondered how a seed could sprout without the necessary nourishment and caring. Despite not receiving any encouragement from his family, Naing decided that he would fly in the teeth of opposition and demonstrate his talents someday. He made up his mind to spend his time reading English books and hone his gift.

He invested his carefully saved pocket money in a stockpile of English books as proof of his determination. His parents resented his pastime; they felt that he was wasting his time and money, and signed him off as a useless airhead.

Naing knew that if he wanted to excel in something, he had to be passionate about staying focused on his goal. That meant that he had to live, breathe, and eat the aspiration to make writing his professional career. It was like pitting one's ambition against the dice of Fate. One wrong move and his dreams would go down the drain. He believed that one needed self-confidence to win this challenge.

In reality it was a slippery slope. At every turn, he faced frustration and despondence. At one point, he nearly gave up.

People with an artistic temperament often falter at crossroads and find it very difficult to get back on their feet. They think their life is miserable and plough the depths of despair. Naing was not an exception to face all these.

* * *

Teenaged Naing improved his English by simply referring to the Oxford dictionary every time he encountered a difficult word. He followed everyone's advice. When someone said to him that he should memorize the entire dictionary, he did his best to do so. It was like the blind leading the blind. He tried every possible way to improve his English, but his efforts were in vain. He needed proper guidance and methods.

During this time, he serendipitously met some people who knew English well. He remembered Mr G Minus who was a master sergeant in the British army and was like a walking dictionary.

They sat on an iron bench at the central train station, and Naing asked Mr Minus for the meaning of some words he hadn't been able to understand when he had read the *Reader's Digest*. Mr Minus readily explained the meanings and Naing was amazed at Mr Minus's vast repertoire of knowledge.

Over a pot of green tea and pea cake, Mr Minus painstakingly explained English vocabulary and grammar to Naing. However, as Mr Minus was weak in Burmese, when he explained new words to Naing, he explained them in English rather than in Burmese. Naing learned a direct method from him and several valuable techniques, including memorizing

words with rhyming patterns, which were used in the olden
education systems.

Another person who significantly contributed to Naing's
English proficiency was a dedicated English grammarian. He
clarified the eight parts of speeches for Naing, establishing
a robust foundation in English grammar. With his clear-cut
explanations, Naing's English was much improved and his
fear of grammar was gone.

Naing knew that most of the English language teachers
in his town relied on widely recognized grammar textbooks
such as, *High School English Grammar* by Wren and Martin,
Nestfield's English Grammar, and *Living English Structure*.

To read all these grammar treatises without a teacher
was akin to cleaning the proverbial Augean stable. So, after
completing his matriculation and his sophomore years, Naing
enrolled in a general English class taught by a renowned
English teacher who preferred American English. While
Naing became adept at American idioms, he still struggled
with constructing a valid sentence because he was clueless
about sentence structures.

* * *

Fortunately, university student Naing encountered another
middle-aged man well-versed in English grammar, a former
headmaster. When the ex-headmaster explained sentence
structure to him, Naing understood the various functions
of English sentences. He specifically utilized the subject and
predicate section of *High School Grammar* to illustrate key
points. It was like the scales fell from his eyes and Naing could
suddenly see the big picture of English sentence construction.

Consequently, he successfully connected the two aspects: the eight parts of speech and composition, effectively bridging his knowledge gap.

Since then, Naing realized that the section on kinds of sentences could serve as a link between the two other parts, especially for those striving to excel in composition. Subsequently, Naing actively sought out rhetoric books to improve his English writing skills. His passion for learning English, tantamount to an obsession, was so profound that he amassed an impressive collection of more than a hundred ELBS English language books.

When he could construct error-free simple sentences, graduate Naing tried to write short stories with the guidance of the books that focused on the art of writing. Gradually, he delved into the realm of creative writing, an area not readily accessible in his town. Recognizing that self-reliance was crucial for achieving his writing goals, he decided that self-study was the only way forward. To enhance both his English proficiency and his writing abilities, he frequented the British Council Library. As he dedicated himself to self-improvement, his writing skills progressed, enabling him to compose short stories in English. From that point forward, he remained steadfast in his determination to write a full-fledged novel when the time was ripe.

* * *

The present novel of author Naing was the fruition of his incessant efforts over a couple of decades. He realized that his dream had materialized in a way. As soon as he completed the draft of his novel, he showed it to the publisher, U Myint, who readily agreed to publish the book in a couple of months. When he excitedly shared this wonderful piece of news with his parents and told them about the contract with the publisher, his father, still keeping to his vow of silence, said nothing. However, Naing knew that his father was rejoicing inwardly to hear the glad tidings of his success.

Naing knew that he needed to work harder if he wanted to become more successful. However, for Naing, success was not the ultimate determinant in his career because he believed in his craft. Whatever the outcome, he would definitely continue to write prolifically and share his views even if there was just a single reader for his literary work.

* * *

At the appointed time on Thursday, Author Naing hailed his friend, Lwin, who was entering the tea shop.

'Hey, Ko Naing, have you been waiting too long?' Lwin smiled at him. Naing proudly handed him an autographed copy of his book. 'Ooh, it's your first novel. I like the title. It makes a lot of sense. It'll definitely be a hit, Naing. I am very proud of you.' Naing smiled.

Just then, the waiter brought them a menu.

'Tea with dumplings,' said Lwin.

Naing also ordered some food and a cup of tea. Naing and Lwin chatted while they waited for their other friends to arrive. They nostalgically reminisced about their carefree, high-school days, recalling the mischief and the unique moments they had shared. They were aware of the importance of preserving those great memories and vowed to cherish them.

For Naing, Sayar Tun's words, 'you have to be crazy when you want to excel in anything' resonated as the gospel truth in his life. Naing had built his life around the motto: where there's a will, there's a way. His life stood as testament to the madness of creative genius, as he successfully accomplished the task he had set for himself: to write a complete novel in English.

In his opinion, he had intrepidly dared to tread the path that few trod upon, and he valued his laurels even though he had not yet reaped the rewards for his labours. His literary debut was successful, and he felt that his efforts had not been in vain for he had pioneered a good example for others like him with high ambitions. Simply put, he had been the torchbearer who had bravely blazed a path for others to follow. He felt pleased with what he had achieved.

In a few days, the book's reviews would appear in local journals, magazines, and even on social media. People would wonder who Writer Naing was and why he chose to write in English rather than in his native language, Burmese. Curiosity would naturally extend to learning more about his life and the efforts behind his work.

Naing's eyes blurred with nostalgia as he remembered Sayar Tun. Just then, more of his friends trooped into the tea shop, greeting and congratulating him before they subsided on to the comfortable chairs and cheerfully chatted with him about his book, *From the Deepest of Heart*.

The Liberated Hairdresser

Hairdresser Ko Tin Maung stared out of a small salon, not because of he found something interesting in the dull street, but because his mind had turned into a void.

Like clockwork, he arrived every morning before 9 a.m. to ensure he could open the hairdressing salon at 9.30 a.m. He could not afford to be late because the salon owner did not tolerate any excuses for tardiness.

His bright, narrow eyes could see the parking area with the private cars basking in the sunlight, yet he showed no interest in the cars. In his apathetic mind, he knew that this innocuous profession was his only career option.

He flinched at the sudden hard grip of a hand on his slender shoulder. He knew instinctively that it was his employer. He had never been treated kindly by this self-centred man ever since he started working here, almost three years ago.

He wallowed in self-pity whenever he thought of his dead-end situation. He didn't enjoy this job and felt life had dealt him an unfair hand when he had been railroaded into this profession.

The owner pocketed sixty per cent of the commissions that Ko Tin Maung earned on haircuts, leaving him with a paltry forty per cent. There had been a verbal agreement and not a written contract regarding the percentage. Ko Tin Maung expended too much of his energy just to pour money into the bottomless pockets of the owner.

Few knew that this kind of bondage still existed in obscure parts of the economically booming town. Even in this competitive and business-minded environment, there were people who exploited the vulnerable.

The careworn hairdresser sighed quietly because he did not want to get into a long-drawn wrangle with his owner, who would attempt to justify the unfair division of the barber's earning as something he did out of mutual interest. Ko Tin Maung wasn't articulate enough to argue with his employer. His face lowered obsequiously and his hands politely clasped behind his back, he asked his red-faced boss what he needed.

The impatient and unsympathetic owner glared at Ko Tin Maung like an angry bull challenging an adversary. 'Don't you have anything to do other than standing there, staring, you lazy lout?' he barked at the hapless barber.

Ko Tin Maung felt humiliated, but he suppressed his rising anger because that kind of an attitude would get him nowhere. Being a devout Buddhist, he knew the law of causality. Perhaps his past life defined his present situation. Patience, according to the religious teachings, was the highest blessing.

'Find something to do—don't just stand there like a useless, inanimate statue. Don't expect anyone to help you when you're in deep shit. You have to rely on yourself. That's my philosophy,' hollered the salon's owner.

Still grumbling to himself, his baggy-trousered employer wobbled out of the salon, probably to have a sumptuous breakfast at the nearby food stall.

Ko Tin Maung had contented himself that morning with a cup of weak and watery tea and a bowl of leftover rice with boiled peas before he had left his humble house in Thanlyin, which was forty-five minutes away from downtown Yangon.

Sometimes he thought what a life he was leading. He felt no better than a living entity that had to eat for survival. He noticed a threadbare broomstick leaning against the worn-out wall and, without any fuss, grasped the broomstick by its handle and started to diligently sweep the floor. He knew that if one were conscientious, one would gain brownie points for good conduct.

He swept the almost-clean floor thoroughly and deliberately, using it as an exercise to calm his anger.

Just as he finished sweeping, a jolly-looking, middle-aged customer in a white shirt came in for a haircut. This man was a regular customer and Ko Tin Maung knew him well.

He greeted his barber, 'Oh, what a stroke of good fortune! There's no one ahead of me for a haircut. Please take your time in cutting my hair.'

It was a routine for him to encounter people from various walks in life in the salon—government officers, labourers, pensioners, children.

Whenever a customer came in for a haircut, Ko Tin Maung knew exactly how to initiate a lively conversation with the customer. First, he wrapped a protective sheet around the customer's neck and draped it over the torso. Funny and amusing dialogues were his stock-in-trade to secure customer loyalty; if not, they would find another place to get their haircut.

The amiable customer initiated a conversation about a neutral topic, 'Have you heard the latest that government employers will get a salary hike?'

Ko Tin Maung nodded and chuckled, 'Yes, I did. If the salaries increase, commodity prices will also get inflated. It's a vicious cycle.'

They both laughed. Out of habit, the hairdresser scraped the stainless-steel scissors on the comb to produce a cheerful clickety-clack sound as he cut hair.

Outside the salon, the street vendor selling Myanmar pancakes sang out his wares to attract people's attention.

'*Baine mote, pu pu lay* (hot pancakes)!'

His strident baritone prompted both of them to look out of the shop. They saw a man, slowly pushing a squalid cart along the street. Now, the baine mote became the subject of their conversation.

'Do you want some baine mote?' asked the customer.

'Not really,' replied Ko Tin Maung, before turning his attention to the unruly hair sprouting behind the man's ear. The customer, now looking at his neat hairstyle in the large, square mirror in front of him, was satisfied with his new look.

The greasy face of the suspicious salon owner popped up in the mirror behind them. After having had a full breakfast, he entered the salon slyly to eavesdrop on the conversation between Ko Tin Maung and the customer. He collapsed heavily into a red plastic chair beside the low table, his ears pricked up to every word being spoken.

As soon as the haircut was done, the hairdresser unwrapped the protective sheet from around the customer's body, shook the hair from it, and draped it over his left arm with a flourish. The satisfied customer ran his fingers through his hair experimentally, beamed and then paid Ks 1,000 to the meticulous hairdresser.

The hairdresser promptly handed over the cash to his employer who snatched it from him and stowed it in the drawer. He bellowed, 'Sweep the floor again before the next customer arrives.'

Saying this, he stretched out his stubby legs, placed them on the table, leaned back in the chair, and shut his eyes. In a few minutes, he was snoring. Ko Tin Maung threw a disgusted glance at his employer and silently began sweeping the floor. His employer's bulging belly rose and fell with every breath. The owner wore a very tight, white T-shirt that was a size too small for him and when he leaned back in the chair, most of his belly was visible. He laced his fingers over his bare potbelly.

Ko Tin Maung cast furtive glances as he swept and scooped up the hair from the floor onto a plastic shovel and dumped them into the dustbin. He replaced the broomstick against the wall and crouched to flip through the periodicals meant for customers awaiting their turn.

He picked up one and began reading it. He found an interesting article about floods in various parts of the country. He was so engrossed in this that he could no longer hear his employer's snoring.

All of a sudden, he heard a loud thud. He looked around to see that his employer had fallen off from the chair. Upset and offended, the fat man stumbled to stand up, but his legs wobbled and failed to support his weight. Ko Tin Maung burst out laughing at his boss's discomfiture.

His fat employer attempted a couple of times to stand up before he was finally successful, albeit a bit shaky. When he stood up, he darted towards Ko Tin Maung and without warning, punched him hard in his face.

The fist smashed him directly on the bridge of his nose. Blood spurted out of Ko Tin Maung's nostrils and spilled on to his white vest, staining it with blotches of red.

Ko Tin Maung's patience had been sorely tested by this bullying and he decided he wouldn't stand it any longer. He picked up the broomstick, twisted off the handle, and hurled it at his fat employer's crew-cut head. A red bulge instantly appeared on his forehead. The owner yelped in pain.

Hearing the commotion, a shocked and surprised neighbour rushed out of his shop next to the salon and peered inside. He saw the employer and the barber wrestling, grappling and hitting each other.

He hollered at them to stop fighting. He shoved the owner away from the hairdresser, who was trying to kick the owner's belly with his skinny legs. The neighbour saw blood on the employer's head and blood on the barber's vest.

'Shame on both of you!'

The fat employer righted the fallen chair and sat down. The hairdresser, his hair ruffled and vest ripped, sat down on the bench, his breathing strenuous. Ko Tin Maung was exasperated.

'I quit. I don't want to work here any more. He isn't human. He's a swine—an animal.'

This time, the employer's eyes bulged with rage, 'What? You dare to call me an animal? You good-for-nothing, lazy lout!'

The fight had now descended into a verbal altercation— abusive, vituperative, and slanderous. The arbitrating neighbour stepped into the fray.

'Stop it, both of you. If not, I'll summon the street official to settle the case.'

Without further ado, Ko Tin Maung snatched his shirt from its hook on the wall and stormed out of the salon, grabbing his red Kachin bag and slinging it over his shoulder along the way.

At long last, he had gotten his freedom and broken free of the verbal bond between the vicious owner and himself. He didn't have to work here any more with this beast in human form. He would find a more suitable place to pursue his profession.

Carefree and light-hearted, he marched down the street. A mouth-wateringly delicious smell assaulted his senses. The recent battle had left him hungry. He dug into his pocket for money, stopped before the cart, and bought some baine mot from the tan-faced hawker.

His first bite of the pancake instantly erased the bitter taste of the tussle in the salon. He relished every bite. He realized just how delicious the pancake was. Without hesitation, he gobbled it all up.

Parallel Lines

It was not as warm as it had been yesterday, but shade was essential for this time of the day—it was almost noon, lunchtime, to be precise. He decided to choose a suitable place to enjoy his al fresco meal.

A table had been laid out under the spreading branches of a short tree. As soon as he sat down, a slim, young waitress approached him and greeted him with a cheerful smile.

'Hi. Good afternoon. How are you? What'll you have for lunch today?'

Being a regular customer, she knew him quite well. She had an open countenance, and like most Myanmar girls, she had applied *thanatkhar*, a natural Myanmar cosmetic, to her face both as a sunscreen and as make-up foundation. She wore a simple outfit: a pink blouse and a red sarong, and her hair had been done up in a pretty hairdo.

He replied with a smile, 'Good afternoon, *nyi-ma-lay* (dear sister). I'd like to have chicken curry and rice.'

She nodded. Within minutes, she served a bowl of chicken curry and a plate of rice; she promised to bring him some vegetables along with fish paste and a bowl of soup. Although it was not his favourite meal, he had to be satisfied with it for he was away from home. At home, he could get a more sumptuous meal than this because his mother was a great cook; but then, beggars can't be choosers.

After she placed the array of dishes before him, he enjoyed his meal in solitary splendour.

He wanted to tease her a little, but he knew that her ever-watchful mother was very strict, and if she suspected him of flirting with her daughter, she would definitely stare him down, and that would put him to shame. There wasn't so much of an age gap between them. He could understand the anxieties of the girl's mother. It was probably with much reluctance that she had placed her daughter in the public eye by asking her to help with the family business.

He had often witnessed the strictures of this feisty woman directed at her hapless daughter, especially when the restaurant brimmed with customers, when she didn't really care about the sensibilities of her patrons. Had it not been for her culinary excellence, her grumbling sometimes grew so unbearable that he would have preferred to stay away from their eatery.

He snapped out of his reverie when the waitress thoughtfully brought him a bottle of cold water and poured it into a glass with a smile. He smiled back warmly at her.

'Please let me know if you need more rice. What did you think of the curry?' Her voice resonated like a silvery chime in his ears and he found himself enchanted by the fragrance of the jasmine flowers she wore in her hair.

'Delicious. The meat is tender.' The customer and the waitress exchanged smiles, blissfully unaware that the girl's shrewish mother was watching them from behind the cash counter.

She called out to her daughter, 'Hey, Hnin, what are you doing standing there? There are other customers to attend to. Stop wasting time!'

Hearing her mother's furious voice, the girl hurried away. He carried on with his meal although he could sense the imminent danger of the storm about to break over his head—the girl's mother would be venting her spleen very soon. Her malicious spite would ruin his appetite.

To pre-empt any disruption to his meal, he ordered two more plates of rice before finishing his meal and drinking all the water from the bottle. Feeling relaxed and satiated, he rubbed his belly. Glancing at his watch, he realized he had another thirty minutes to kill before his friend arrived at around 12.30 p.m. He stood up.

He leaned back in the plastic chair and reached for the plastic box that contained the lump of jaggery that was served as dessert. As he chewed on it, he saw people entering and leaving the food stall. He made a mental note of their attire and bearing.

He noticed some plums tastefully displayed in a barrow beside him. It was sort of an advertisement for this special kind of a plum that was very famous in Myanmar because it came all the way from Salay, a city in upper Myanmar. As it was seedless, the entire fruit could be eaten as a snack and he loved it.

It was gradually getting hotter as the sun rose higher. He watched a toddler in a ragged and dirty vest playing happily

in the street beside the barrow. He envied the child's carefree
life. The child's mother sat washing some plums in a plastic
bucket of water. Every now and then, she looked across at
her near-naked baby girl. As a mother, she was both watchful
and cheerful.

In life, it is imperative to have a roof over one's head for
refuge and shade. Of the various kinds of shades, the coolest
and safest was the one provided by the mother. Even a hen
protects her chicks beneath her wings and fiercely fights any
danger that threatens them.

The very thought warmed the cockles of his heart. He
understood the value of shade and refuge for every life
form—they were probably the most precious things in life
because every living creature seeks these; some are successful,
some are not. At that particular point in time, he enjoyed the
shade of the tree that protected him from the blistering heat
of the sun.

To his right were two young maidens at a table, presumably
having lunch, although he wasn't sure if they had ordered any
food. They attracted his attention because they seemed to be
roughly the same age as he was. One of them held the very
latest model in mobile phones. Mobile phones had become
an integral part of everyday life.

A few minutes later, the girl with the cell phone walked
into the parking lot, seemingly engaged in a business call or
something similar. The other girl sat alone at the table, looking
at her friend's back. She appeared apathetic, while the girl
with the phone seemed animatedly engaged in conversations.

He observed every movement made by the girl with
the mobile phone. A few minutes ticked by. An expensive
sedan pulled into the parking lot in front of the restaurant.

The driver said something to the girl with the phone, who then turned and signalled to her friend to join them. They both got into the car.

Meanwhile, some people scattered crumbs for a flock of pigeons, but the sedan honked as it drove away, startling the birds into flight.

* * *

Watching the pigeons soar gracefully into the air took his mind back to his home. He remembered his mother's parting words before he left for Yangon to do business: 'Son, you know when you go there, you'll have to depend only on yourself. You could meet someone who could give you what could sound like good advice, but they could lead you astray. You have to always prioritize what matters and what doesn't. You have to use your common sense without blindly following someone else's advice. Be clear in your mind about your own ambitions and strive to achieve them. I know you want to become a successful writer, so you have to do your best to attain it, without letting your mind get distracted. Keep trying and believe in your dream, son.'

His mother's words, engraved on his psyche, kept him grounded and provided the necessary shade and support to move ahead in his life. They also fuelled the fire in his belly, propelling him to succeed in his career. His mother's unwavering support helped him understand the depth of a parent's love and care. This not only served as a foundation to springboard the child's career but also gave the child the freedom and space to make his own decisions, live happily, and prosper.

His parents' words were beacons to guide him and keep him on the straight and narrow, steering clear of human folly. Youngsters often feel adventurous and take shortcuts or diversions just to experience the thrill of exploring something new or prohibited. They leave the shade of their parents without caring much for the dangers that lie ahead.

It was the greatest measure of the sincere and boundless parental love to allow their children to leave the nest in pursuit of their own fortune. Reflecting on this, he gulped down another cup of water and felt a bit relieved. He watched the woman who sold plums cuddle her child, tenderly rubbing her nose on the child's cheek. Her face was radiant with love and happiness as the toddler in her arms chuckled and cooed at her touch.

A warmth arose in his heart as he thought of his own mother, whom he missed deeply. She always took care of him whenever he needed her and was his genuine shade and refuge. He paid homage to her image in his mind. She was a source of comfort to him, and he wished everyone in the world would possess such a shade and refuge.

The scene of a mother and child enhanced his belief in parental love more than before. He was sure that only parental love could beautify the world and create a kinder, more loving environment for everyone.

He murmured, 'Mom, you are my true refuge and shade. I will do my utmost to repay you with my gratitude, although this is a debt that could never be fully repaid.' His face grew radiant as he smiled, outshining the sun overhead.

Redemption

Home is where the heart is, although it is not always easy to establish a home where every member of the household loves, protects, understands, and supports the other. Such a family would experience ultimate bliss. If not . . .

Min Hla Oo, aged thirty-five, pondered deeply about this because he felt like a misfit—suffocated and trapped in his parents' home, despite having lived here for nearly four decades. No one paid any heed to his opinions or ideas; in fact, his family disparaged him. He felt very hurt about being at the receiving end of such shoddy treatment. He wanted to find his own space and wondered how to move out.

His family felt that Min Hla Oo ought not to rock the boat and make unnecessary and abrupt changes because that would be tantamount to shooting himself in the foot.

Min Hla Oo never wrongfully blamed anyone because he loved and cherished his family. He lived with three older sisters and his parents—six members in all, including himself. Their family owned a bookshop. Min Hla Oo loved books. He hoped to make a career in maintaining the family business.

In the cut-throat rat race of today's world, he realized that running a family business in the old-fashioned way would be difficult for survival. They would need to modernize. He underwent training in a local business school, which provided the rudimentary foundation for future entrepreneurs.

When he aired his views, his dad scowled at Min Hla Oo and bluntly said, 'No. No way. Although I know you're right, don't expect me to change how I do things here.'

Unwilling to stir the hornet's nest, Min Hla Oo fell silent. He wondered why he and his father could never concur on anything; why were they so different and always at loggerheads? This idea would benefit his whole family, but his father dismissed it out of hand as being too theoretical and impractical. According to his father, the only thing that would help one survive in business was hard work. However, Min Hla Oo believed that it was good management. Again, on this very point, they did not see eye to eye.

Whenever there was a problem with his parents' shop, Min Hla Oo attempted to resolve their issues by quoting inspiring examples of their neighbouring shops, which ran smoothly under excellent management. He pointed out that their neighbours had modernized and their businesses ran like well-oiled machines.

As always, no one agreed with him. One of his sisters went so far as to say, 'Yeah, I know, but they're doing it their way and we want to do it our way.'

Hence, one could only say that as a family, they were very obstinate. That's why whenever Min Hla Oo wanted to convey something to his father, he first spoke to his mother, who would share it with her husband during their dinner-table discussions, the time reserved for addressing filial and family matters.

Min Hla Oo usually ate alone in the kitchen without anyone talking to him or making dinner for him. He naturally felt very lonely living in this family.

His daily morning routine clearly demonstrated his estrangement from his family, even though they all lived under the same roof. Every morning, as soon as he woke up, he would go to the nearby tea shop for breakfast. However, on some days, he had his morning meal at home when his mom kindly made him his favourite fried-rice dish and tea. However, she would have no time to chat with her son at this time because she would be in a bustle getting ready to go grocery shopping at the nearest market to fix a meal for the rest of the family.

After his breakfast, he joined some friends at their regular haunt, the tea shop, and talked about business. He was specifically learning about the publishing business from his friends who were thriving in this field. The discovery of a good and successful author in the contemporary field was akin to striking gold in their line of business.

He gained this kind of insight from some of his peers, through whom he befriended several writers. The authors approached him to showcase their works for potential publication. He needed to raise some capital to take their books to print.

When he talked about this to his mother, she rained on his parade and warned Min Hla Oo that he would be cheated by these fair-weather friends, 'Look, honey, they will swindle you 'cos I know that they are just looking for someone whom they can fleece.'

He felt very let down by his mother's attitude towards his business strategies and realized that she didn't support his future career in the publishing industry. Disheartened and in despair, he dumped his vast book collection into a dark corner of his room where they lay haplessly, gaping at him in bewilderment.

After this happened repeatedly, he decided to leave his parents' house. Using some of his carefully saved pocket money, he established his own publishing business and earned from translating some humorous English tales into Myanmar.

Although they knew what he was doing, he didn't discuss his business with his family and did it all in his own way. Soon, he got himself a network of friends in the same business.

Suddenly and miraculously, his life changed. Unexpectedly he fell in love with a girl about his own age. Her name was Mu Mu. She was the sister of his friend Ko Thar. Once again, he found it difficult to discuss his romantic affair with his family members because they were conservative and set in their ways.

He felt that through gentle persuasion he could eventually overcome this hurdle. He took the bull by the horns and asked his parents for their consent to his alliance.

Fortunately, he did this with conviction and his parents demonstrated their generosity by arranging a separate apartment for the newly-weds. Now, as the breadwinner of the family, he had to stand on his own feet. He understood that he was the one who could make improvements in his lifestyle and that this was the acid test for his theories about running a business.

He did his job independently and well. He even mentored those who wanted to learn English from him. He was doing very well indeed and his parents and siblings now respected his efforts and success. His wife supported him unfailingly, providing him with energy and stamina. He knew that life in publishing business was not a cakewalk, but he firmly believed that as long as one worked hard, one could survive in this world.

A year went by and he had a cute kid who looked a lot like him. Whenever he held his son, he saw the future in the child and his heart overflowed with warmth and happiness. Now that he had his own little family to share his life with, it didn't mean that he would be ungrateful to his parents and sisters. They too demonstrated their love for him in their own ways.

His filial duty was still incomplete. He decided to help manage and expand his parents' business now that he could stand on his own feet with the invaluable support of his own family, especially his beloved wife. This was a test of his ability, capacity, and creativity. At long last, he felt safe and secure in his home. He was the lord of the manor and king of his castle, and able to make his decisions and follow them through to fruition. He felt a real sense of accomplishment as a family man. Furthermore, he had gotten back his estranged family. He could definitely say that he was finally home.

Under the Bright Sunlight

As soon as the ferry docked at Dala jetty across the Yangon River, its passengers were eager to get off the barge, reminiscent of wild stallions unleashed from their stalls. Oo joined the stampede. A middle-aged man in the faded-red, grubby, and worn Adidas hat approached him just then and asked him hesitantly if he needed a trishaw.

The man's weather-beaten hat still performed its duty, protecting him from the sun and the rain. The man's stained shirt was fastened with a single button, revealing the bony ribcage of his chest. He had the appearance of a typical trishaw driver in his ankle-length, black-and-red-chequered longyi, which bared his hairy shins.

Oo realized that the man with the sweaty, brown face was looking for a passenger. Indicating the solidly built, corrugated-roofed ticket-office, the man said he had a trishaw parked near the building. 'Please take a ride on my trishaw, *a ko* (brother). I will take you to wherever you want to go. I won't charge you much.'

The man's eyes seemed to beseech him to come with him. Oo nodded to the man, who immediately made a way through the crowd for Oo, and said, 'This way, a ko.'

They walked through the crowd to the trishaw and tok-tok stand on the street that led to the main road of the city from the jetty. On the way to the parked trishaw, Oo saw food vendors, a betel-quid seller, a sliced-watermelon seller, and many other hawkers.

Oo noticed that the betel-quid shop was surrounded by men, both young and old, waiting for their turn to be served. The vendor was busy wrapping betel leaves as quickly as he could, smearing the leaves with a little bit of lime and cutch, adding tobacco, aniseed, and shredded chunks of betel nuts.

A man spat out betel 'blood' onto the pavement and the red juice almost splattered over Oo. The man grinned and apologized for his carelessness. 'Sorry, a ko. I did not notice you approach.'

Almost immediately, the man seemed to forget his indiscretion and resumed his conversation with his friend. Oo knew that this was one of those disgusting habits found in the city, where people chewed betel and carelessly spat the betel juice onto the pavements, making the whole city hideous.

* * *

In the olden days, the quay bustled with vendors who sold fries, boiled duck eggs and quail eggs, or seasonal fruit such as mangoes, durians, and so on. Oo's friend had told him that these former vendors had now become water fetchers to earn their living. After the upgrade of the quay structure, new safety procedures had been enforced and the vendors were no longer allowed to sell their goods on the quay or on the boats.

* * *

The sun shone down mercilessly, making people blink; it also weighed Oo down, but he shrugged it off, looking up at the cloudless sky, nonchalantly.

* * *

As a lad, Oo had visited Dala city along with his friends during the summer holidays. He had seen people rent out comics and magazines to the boat passengers to help them kill time on the way to Dala.

Others shouted out their wares, which included *Bilatyay*, a soft drink like orangeade or lemon soda, easily available these days. In those days, the vendors mixed coloured powder with water to make these soft drinks. They were very popular with the kids.

His thoughts paused and suddenly wandered back to his recent trip on the ferry. He had been seated on a plastic chair for which he'd had to pay Ks 300. He scanned the Yangon River, which had the colour of a latte—its current carrying drifting coconuts and fronds down to the mouth of the river.

* * *

The refreshing breeze across the river caressed his brow. He had been so busy photographing the things he saw in front of him that he missed noticing the circling seagulls over the bow of the boat as it left the Pansodan Jetty to Dala.

He saw the towering buildings and cranes of the industrial ports from the boat's deck. The famous port authority building with its tall tower stood out in their midst. He remembered that its architect, Oliphant, was one of the famous architects who designed landmark buildings in downtown Rangoon.

* * *

Before the ferry left the jetty, Oo saw some dark-skinned vendors near the ticket office selling guavas, plums (sweet and sour or spicy), and water chestnuts.

Having been up since early that morning, he planned to make Dala his next writing spot and decided to go there via the jetty. He wanted a new topic—something weighty like an article piece about the socio-economic life of the people of Dala.

* * *

As soon as the whistle blew, the barge gradually pulled out of the jetty, emitting smoke from its chimney and sounding its horn several times to warn latecomers that it was leaving the jetty. The latecomers hurriedly made their way, some waving frantically to catch the attention of friends or family already on board. On both decks, people sat on wooden benches neatly arranged in a row.

The scene was filled with a sense of anticipation and activity as the barge, now slowly gaining momentum, seemed to respond to the urgency of the departing signal. The rhythmic churning of the water beneath the barge, mirrored the excitement in the air. The smoke billowing from the chimney created a hazy backdrop, adding a touch of drama to the departure.

Oo noticed special seats reserved for tourists. They seemed more comfortable than the seats for local passengers and he felt this was an unfair discrimination against the locals. He consoled himself that the difference was probably because of the higher rates set for foreign passengers—100 kyats for local passengers and 3,000 kyats for foreign passengers. The atmosphere on both decks buzzed with a sense of adventure and the unknown, as the barge forged ahead, leaving the jetty behind in its wake.

* * *

Oo saw people flocking in and out of the ticket building. He also noticed the newly renovated bridges that led passengers to the landing. Dala city appeared to have undergone significant changes. This impression intensified when he noticed newly paved roads in every quarter.

When Oo had visited Dala city in his youth, it had been nothing like this. The port town seemed to have boomed and gotten a lot more developed. He saw cars and motorbikes speeding about. Some of them called out to the disembarking passengers, asking them whether they wanted a ride to Kawt Muu, Kone Chan Kone, Twente, and other neighbouring towns.

* * *

When the trishaw man led him to his vehicle, Oo woke up from his stupor and decided to visit the centre of the town. It was his habit to visit the town centre whenever he visited a new place, whether on business or vacation.

When he stepped out of the building, he saw that the road was flanked by rows of restaurants and tea shops. The street led to the famous clocktower that served as the central point of the town. The trishaw man asked him where he wanted to go.

'I want to go around the city, but take me to the clocktower first.' The trishaw man nodded.

The local market squares were strategically positioned around the impressive, red clocktower. It was the busiest place in the city and Oo decided that this was where he could study the local people's lifestyle.

* * *

He asked the trishaw man to stop at the entrance of the market, where the vendors bustled about, setting up their stalls. People carrying plastic baskets ambled in and out of the marketplace, which was a hive of commercial activity. After a few minutes, Oo asked the trishaw man to carry on with his tour of the city.

* * *

Oo suddenly changed his mind and said, 'Can you take me to your place?'

Surprised by this unusual request, the trishaw man replied without hesitation, 'I don't mind taking you to my place, a ko. I'm but a poor man, so my place may not be good enough to welcome you.'

* * *

Half an hour later, the trishaw man stopped in front of a small compound, surrounded by tall coconut trees, a shabby hut with a thatched roof at the centre. The old man pointed to his humble abode and said, 'Here we are. This is my house, a ko.'

He dismounted from his trishaw and gestured to Oo to step down. Stooping low as a sign of respect, the trishaw man led Oo into his dwelling. Inside, Oo saw a small shrine against a rattan wall. Beneath it lay a pile of pillows and blankets, which seemed worn and tattered.

* * *

A young boy emerged from the kitchen to welcome the trishaw man, who whispered something to the kid, who retreated into the kitchen again. When the lad reappeared, he was leading a man by the hand. The trishaw man asked the man to bring a pot of green tea for Oo, who had sat down cross-legged, placing his bag beside him.

Oo looked around the hut and observed that, despite sunlight streaming in through the small gaps in the rattan wall, it remained relatively dim inside. The trishaw man poured the green tea into two cups—one for Oo and the other for himself. He blew at the steam rising from the cup, took a sip and then replaced it on the tray.

Oo also took a sip and initiated the conversation.

The trishaw man said, 'As you know, a ko, we live a hand-to-mouth existence, depending on our daily income to secure food, clothing, and shelter. If we don't work even for a single day, our rice bowl will be empty. Therefore, there is no rest day for us, except when we are very ill and then, we call it a day for relaxation.'

During this conversation, the boy sat beside the trishaw man and looked up at his face every now and then, almost as if he were waiting for a reply.

'Ah, as you can see, the child's mother, my wife, has been hospitalized, and I've had to call my cousin to babysit him while I ply my trishaw to earn money.'

The little boy continued playing with a broken toy car.

* * *

Oo asked him questions about his family and neighbours.

'All have the same sentiment. Our aspirations aren't that lofty. We don't expect to live in swanky hotels or own expensive cars. We simply hope for a modest, frugal life without the constant worry about our daily earnings.'

Oo was deeply moved by the trishaw man's honesty. These people didn't expect much; they only desired a simple and peaceful life. As long as they lived without worries, they were satisfied.

Oo sympathized with the man's philosophy in life. He believed that there could be a way for them to improve their situation. However, until they found a solution, life would remain as it always had.

Oo spent nearly forty-five minutes at the trishaw man's humble house, gaining insights into the way people lived in this part of the city. Then he remembered an appointment he had made for that afternoon in Yangon.

He glanced at the trishaw man's straightforward and determined face. The man asked Oo, 'A ko, do you want to still see the clocktower? I can take you there.'

Oo shook his head, 'No. Please take me back to the jetty. I need to return to Yangon.'

The trishaw paddler did as he was told and took him back to the jetty.

Lost in reverie, Oo wondered whether there was any truth in the popular belief that hopes and dreams could uplift a man's mentality or spirit from the turmoil of life.

All this while, the trishaw man was pedalling with all his might to reach the jetty in time before the barge left for Pansodan jetty in half an hour. The sun shone brightly overhead, without concern for the people below and performed its duty of giving light to people.

22

The Enigma of Big Bunny's Arrival

It was his habit to frequent a Chinese tea shop near the famous Bogyoke Market, previously called Scott Market. The city had transformed significantly to keep pace with the country's progress in the global market. Numerous new bistros and restaurants had mushroomed throughout the city, all competing to attract a diverse array of customers and consumers.

However, he held a preference for this particular tea shop, which seemed well-maintained, less shoddy, and more inviting than the other cafés. Renowned for its excellent tea and a wide variety of dumplings and Chinese snacks, the eatery stood out from the rest. Since it was almost noon, there were only a few patrons, a deliberate choice on his behalf. Feeling famished, he decided a cup of tea and a dumpling would be just what the doctor ordered. Upon arrival, he chose to sit at a corner table where he would be undisturbed and allowed to ponder. At the counter, a kettle and some snacks idled, awaiting customers.

He would often find himself seated at this tea shop whenever he needed to think or read, sometimes purely to enjoy the solitude, and at other times for the simple pleasure of sipping tea. What drew him to this spot was the absence of disturbances, allowing him to drink his tea peacefully. With each quiet sip, he could reflect on things, finding the refreshing taste of tea invigorating his mind. The waiters here knew him well, because he was a regular patron.

The owner of the establishment scowled darkly whenever one of the waiters spoke to the protagonist, clearly resenting friendships between waiters and the customers.

He understood that some waiters, in an attempt to defraud their employer, used the old trick of announcing amounts with substantial deductions from the real cost of the bill rather than reporting the actual cost of the drinks. The owner's business was, thus, adversely affected by disloyal employees.

The protagonist ordered a cup of tea from a young waiter whose eyes drooped with exhaustion. Perhaps he had stayed up the previous night for the Premier League. Many youngsters loved to watch football games, even at the cost of their precious sleep. The protagonist smiled at the waiter, who silently took his order and turned to leave.

The protagonist stopped him and asked for a pen because he wanted to create a to-do list for the errands he needed to run at home. The waiter returned shortly with a pen for him and told him that he could return it when he was done writing.

As he fumbled to extract a piece of paper from his pocket, he accidentally knocked the pen off the table. He gasped and groaned at his clumsiness as the pen dropped to the floor. He wondered what was happening to him these days. The writer's block was probably due to the huge amount of work at home causing fatigue that left him enervated.

As he fumbled around under the table looking for his pen, he touched something velvety. Intrigued, he wondered what it could be. Was it a piece of carpet or something else? His curiosity piqued, he picked it up from the floor and his jaw dropped as he found himself holding a long, white ear in his hand.

A pair of wide, red eyes stared at him intently, causing him to hold his breath. *Oh, no!* It was a white rabbit. The trembling creature uttered a few words, which he couldn't understand at first. However, as he looked at its lips, he was able to decipher its language.

'I . . . my name is Big Bunny. Please don't hurt me,' the frightened bunny rabbit spoke softly.

The protagonist pitied the harmless creature and assured it that he meant no harm. Gently, he placed it on the chair beside him. Strangely enough, the rabbit was invisible to others, which was fortunate. He wanted to feed the rabbit but wasn't sure what it would eat. He was fairly certain that rabbits were vegetarians. All he had were dumplings and some pea cake, which wouldn't be suitable for a rabbit's diet.

He whispered to the rabbit, 'Where do you come from?'

The rabbit looked like it was lost in deep thought, and did not hear anything. In reality, some events unfolded in its mind.

* * *

The rabbit remembered that day vividly. As it had been a moonless night, the place had been pitch dark. Its duty was to accompany the old man only on nights with a full moon. Consequently, on moonless nights, it had the leisure to loiter around here and there. Since it was the rabbit's night off, the old man would not mind.

However, when the rabbit invited the old man to play a game of hide-and-seek, he rudely refused, using his old age as an excuse, and also said something insulting to the bunny. Being naughty, the bunny ignored the old man's refusal and insisted he played.

The old man repeatedly rebuffed the bunny, until the vexed creature grew sullen and then it hopped away to play by itself not caring about whether the old man would worry about its sudden absence. The old man didn't know that the rabbit had a very obstinate nature.

The stubborn bunny played very happily in solitude among some scattered rocks. Although it loved to play hide-and-seek, the game required a friend. Feeling sorry for itself, it cavorted around solo, until finally, it fell asleep out of exhaustion.

Suddenly, a loud whirring jolted the rabbit awake. It saw something indescribable descending onto the surface of the moon. Soon, the strange vehicle's door opened and a stranger emerged. The rabbit wasn't sure whether it was happening for real or if he was dreaming because the stranger wore a weird, shiny outfit. It had never seen such a person before on this planet. Petrified, it became rigid and motionless. It just stared at the man with wide eyes.

When the curious-looking stranger espied the bunny, he came over to it. He quickly scanned the surroundings and saw nothing ominous but the rocks. Glad that there was no danger, he bent down, picked up the bunny and held it very gently. As a matter of fact, he tried to cuddle it like a pet because he was such a good-hearted man.

The bunny was so terrified that, although it trembled, it didn't dare to move for fear that the man might inadvertently hurt it. The rabbit shut its eyes, pretending to fall asleep. Believing that the bunny was asleep, the kindly stranger gently put it down beside the big rock, careful not to disturb it from its slumber, and then went away to complete his mission.

The sly bunny, still pretending to be fast asleep, saw the strange spaceship that had landed near a rock about five yards away. The vehicle had a flag of some sort on it, although the bunny couldn't identify which country it represented—it just saw some stars and stripes and its peculiar shape resembled that of a big cone. The bunny assumed that the man had flown here in it.

A few minutes later, the man returned from wherever he had gone. Through the visor of his helmet, he greeted the bunny warmly, because he saw that it was now awake. Surprised to find that the man seemed so amiable and friendly, the rabbit lost its fear.

He gave the bunny something to eat and it tasted delicious. The bunny quickly gobbled it all up because all that playing had made it tired and hungry. Suddenly, a thought struck the rabbit: this man was so much kinder and sympathetic towards the little bunny unlike the old man with whom it currently lived.

The rabbit concluded that the old man was not a true friend because he scolded the cute bunny rabbit all the time and never provided it with any food. In a childish tantrum, it contemplated all the undesirable traits of the old man.

Soon, the stranger and the bunny became good friends—no more fear, no more worries. They chatted for hours. The man asked the bunny some questions, and it replied in detail—mostly lamenting about the hard and lonely life it was forced to lead. Although the spaceman listened attentively and sympathized with the poor rabbit's plight, when it was time for him to return to his spaceship, which was waiting to take him home, he couldn't take the bunny with him.

Before he left, the man whispered something to the bunny. Nobody knew what the man said to the bunny. The day was imprinted very clearly in its mind.

* * *

When the bunny woke up from its reverie, he replied calmly to its enthusiastic interrogator, 'I belong to the Myanmar traditions and legends; not the Greek mythology, which is full of gods and goddesses. I'm Big Bunny from the moon.'

It paused here, perhaps wanting to gather up its courage.

His captivated audience implicitly believed Big Bunny's tale because he had heard this story as a child, as told by his grandmother. Whenever the moon was full, his grandmother sat on the porch of their house, holding him in her lap and recounted this fable as was the custom of the people of Myanmar.

'I'll bring some oiled rice in a golden plate from the moon, in which you will see an old man and a rabbit. The man is pounding the rice in the mortar, with his rabbit sitting beside him,' said grandmother.

He wondered where the old man was and why the bunny was here all by itself? Did they have a falling out? Surely, the poor old man would miss his furry little companion, he thought. He asked Big Bunny why it had run away from the old man.

Did they have a quarrel? Oh! the poor old man!

He sighed, saddened by this thought, and then glanced at Big Bunny, who gazed at him in puzzlement.

He felt that he ought to try and persuade the rabbit to return to the moon. If not, the legend wouldn't hold true for the next generation, and children wouldn't be able to see the old man with his bunny in the moon. The whole tradition would be lost forever; something very detrimental for Myanmar children. Such stories and traditions ought to be preserved for posterity.

The interlocutor's final question to Big Bunny was about the purpose of its visit. Aware that the man would find its tale implausible, it took the rabbit a while to recount its story, adhering closely to the truth because honesty was always the best policy for everyone. It was one of the homilies that the old man had often imparted to Big Bunny. At this point, personal peeves did not come into the picture.

'When the astronaut Armstrong landed on the moon, he invited me to come to Earth whenever I felt like it. Upon his warm invitation, I visited Earth and came in peace. I'm not running away from the old man. Don't worry, my friend I will go back to the moon where I was born.'

The bunny's answer was convincing because it understood the man's concern well. As soon as the rabbit came to the end of its story, it vanished into thin air, like it had never been there. The man felt like a weight had been lifted from his shoulders and was happy to have personally experienced such an incredible incident in his lifetime. Nevertheless, he needed to do a reality check, and for that purpose, he needed to wait for nightfall when the moon would appear.

The protagonist knew that he needed to be patient in some cases, especially this one. In the meantime, he drained the dregs in the teacup—the taste was marvellous. He felt fresh and rejuvenated. At that moment, his grandma's words echoed in his head. He silently thanked his grandma for her efforts to instil the cultural reverence for one's own tradition and customs in him, without which he could not be a true-blue folklore lover; or the commitment to propagate one's own culture would not survive. It has to pass from generation to generation. It is the bounden duty of every citizen.

A mental image flashed in his mind of the old man with his rabbit in the silvery moon. He closed his eyes and relaxed.

23

A Father's Sincere Wish

Firmly gripping the veranda's balustrade with his wrinkled hands, U Ba Win, with weary eyes, harked back to those days when his family thrived, prospered, and was happy. Everyone in his circle envied him for his perfect life—having a good, competent wife and a beautiful, intelligent daughter.

In front of him were some mango and coconut trees, and there were cars parked in the street—all of which depicted a quiet ambience. As was their morning routine, the crows cawed raucously, while the sparrows pecked at grains in birdfeeders that dangled from the branch of a tree.

A little boy was giggling happily, playing with his toy in the street. The boy stumbled often due to his weak legs. The kid's concerned mom kept a close eye on him to ensure that he didn't fall down and end up with bruises or injuries.

Looking at the scene, U Ba Win felt warmth in his heart and his mind wandered back into the past. He, his wife, Tin, and his only daughter, Sabai, lived happily in a

flat on the first floor of a public housing complex in the
suburb of Yangon.

It was now almost a year since Sabai, their daughter,
had left them for good. They could not bring themselves to
believe that their child had departed from the world ahead
of them. She could have lived longer than that, but fate
arbitrarily took her away from her parents.

Sabai was a well-mannered girl, nurtured with care by both
her parents. An outstanding student, she consistently earned
accolades and prizes from her early years. Throughout her
school days, she had unfailingly ranked among the class toppers.

When she passed her matriculation, despite achieving
six distinctions, she aspired to pursue arts and science with
a major in history. During this period, U Ba Win, her father,
wanted her to got to medical school and eventually become
a doctor. A disagreement ensued, leading her to avoid her
father, and communication ceased between them. For almost
a year after that, she spoke only to her mother, and the
relationship between father and daughter remained strained.
He finally relented and gave in to Sabai's decision.

During his daughter's final days, U Ba Win found it
unbearable to watch his daughter's the pain and suffering.
Despite her illness, Sabai had displayed remarkable resilience
until then. His wife had been a pillar of support for their
daughter and had sat by her bedside, reading sacred texts to
her. Sabai's parents held the belief that she would be reborn
in a better realm because of the merits she had accrued in
her present life.

* * *

U Ba Win vividly remembered the day when his daughter, Sabai, came into the world. When his wife started to bleed, they had rushed to the women's hospital in a taxi. That night at the hospital, he had been like a cat on a hot tin roof, anxiously waiting for the baby to arrive. Unaware of the baby's gender at the time, he decided that he would be happy whether it was a boy or a girl. He would love it because he was the father.

His wife went into labour at midnight. U Ba Win kicked his heels in the corridor, repeatedly glancing at the labour ward's closed doors and then checking the time on his watch. He stood by the tall windows, gazing out at the surroundings. The neon lights on the lamp posts around the hospital's compound were still visible; soon, it would be dawn. Other expectant mothers were wheeled into the ward and emerged triumphantly with their babies, but it was only in the morning that Sabai was born.

His wife's sister-in-law arrived at the hospital very early that morning and took matters into her capable hands, 'Don't worry too much, Ko Ba Win,' she said, 'this delay is fairly common, especially when a woman delivers her first baby. I too had the same experience. Believe me, next time, it'll be much easier.'

Unfazed by the sterile hospital atmosphere, she peeped into the labour room, saw a nurse, and strolled in to chat with her.

She returned to Ko Ba Win and said, 'Your wife's delivery is quite difficult but the doctors and nurses are taking good care of her. So don't worry; she's in good hands and she'll deliver the child very soon.'

His anxiety intensified when the tick of the watch grew louder with the passage of time. He looked at the watch again, 8.30 a.m.

He sprang forward as a nurse emerged through the doors and called his name, 'Is Ko Ba Win here? Your wife gave birth to a daughter weighing over six pounds. Mother and child are healthy, but it took longer than expected. The baby has a rapid heartbeat, so we'll need to take her into the ICU. Please follow me.'

He threw a glance at his wife's sister-in-law and hurried after the nurse. She brought a gurney on which his little daughter had been laid. The child gazed at him with the brightest eyes he had ever seen. He had never seen such a beautiful baby before. He felt quite wonderful. His heart swelled with an indescribable feeling. The infant was so beautiful and looked just like her mother.

With the feeling of fatherhood coursing through him, he felt inordinately proud as he kept pace with the trolley being wheeled by two paramedics towards the ICU. When they arrived at the double doors of the intensive care unit, they took the child inside and told him that he would need to come back to collect his baby after three days. He was reluctant to leave the room, but he needed to check on his wife in the labour ward. She would need his support and encouragement.

* * *

Sabai was a well-behaved girl even as a child. U Ba Win and his wife instilled in her the basic teachings of Buddhism as well as her filial duties. She grew up to be an obedient student with her teachers and a good friend to her friends. People praised U Ba Win's good fortune to have such a wonderful daughter.

* * *

U Ba Win had a flashback of the awards ceremony of his daughter's kindergarten days. The auditorium was filled to the rafters and the girl who won the first prize in her exam was the cynosure of all eyes. It was Sabai, smiling broadly on the stage as she graciously received her prize from the headmistress.

They took a group photo after the event. His wife gifted her clever daughter a beautiful dress for making them the proudest parents in the school and U Ba Win bought her a pretty doll. Sabai was overjoyed and kissed both her parents. She treasured that dress and kept it as a keepsake even after she reached adulthood.

* * *

He grew misty-eyed just thinking about his beloved daughter and whispered, 'Why did you have to leave us so early, my dear? You should be with us.'

Just then, he heard his wife's feeble voice call out to him from the bedroom. She was bedridden, grappling with the challenges of senile dementia. She wanted *congee* for her breakfast.

He hurried back into the apartment. When his wife saw him, she reached out to touch him. He knew that she wanted to say something. Without compelling her to speak, he nodded, indicating that he understood and would attend to her needs right away. He sat on the edge of her bed and gently patted both her hands.

He looked at her eyes tenderly and said, 'I'll buy you some congee, my dear. I'll be back in a few minutes.'

He took out a stainless-steel container from the kitchen cupboard, from which he carefully extracted two 1,000-kyat notes to buy the congee. He pulled on his white shirt and went out, closing the door behind him gently.

* * *

In the street, he heard the gleeful chuckling of the little boy, who was now astride a tricycle while his young mother helped propel it forward by pushing it from behind. When they saw him, the young mother waved to him, 'Good morning, Uncle, where are you going?'

U Ba Win replied, 'Good morning, my dear. Just around the corner of the street for some congee for your auntie.'

'All right, Uncle. Please let me know if I can help you with anything.'

He nodded and smiled at her as she returned to her duty of pushing the cycle along the street. The little boy whooped with glee as his tiny vehicle gathered speed.

At the congee shop, U Ba Win specifically ordered carp congee instead of the usual chicken congee. He waited as the vendor filled a container with congee, and when the seller handed it to him, he paid the man two 1,000-kyat notes. The seller returned a 500-kyat note because a bowl of congee was 1,500 kyats.

When U Ba Win returned to his house with the congee, the child was still pedalling his tricycle, his mother behind him. U Ba Win smiled at them and nodded when the young mother called out, 'Uncle, please tell Auntie that I'll drop by to see this evening.'

U Ba Win walked up a few flights of stairs to his flat with the container of steaming-hot congee, which emitted a mouth-watering aroma. In the kitchen, he carefully transferred the contents of the container into a porcelain bowl. He put a porcelain spoon in the bowl and carried it to his wife.

Sitting beside her, he gently adjusted her position, raising her to a semi-recumbent state. He blew into the bowl of congee several times to release the heat before ladling a spoonful into his wife's mouth. She gulped it down gratefully. After a few spoons of the broth, she decided that she'd had enough.

He wiped her mouth with a napkin and smiled at her. She drank the water he offered her, before lying back on her pillow again. When she closed her eyes, he understood that he should leave her to relax. He went into the sitting room to do some reading.

He looked around and found that day's newspaper. Sitting down in a comfortable armchair, he read an interesting article in the paper about Myanmar's classical music—the Myanmar Drum ensemble that was his favourite kind of music.

* * *

He looked at the clock on the wall—1.45 p.m. He decided to take a quick power nap before starting to fix dinner and lay down on the couch in the living room. Within a few minutes, he fell into a deep sleep and dreamt of his daughter.

His wife and daughter wept before he left for his posting in a town in Upper Myanmar. He assured them that they would see him again, real soon—as soon as he had settled down in a comfortable place—and that he would return to Yangon and take them back with him. They couldn't join him just then because Sabai's final examination was fast approaching.

On the night before he left, as he sat reading a magazine, his daughter emerged from her room, holding something behind her back. She approached him and said, 'Daddy, I know that Upper Myanmar has a cold climate. Here's something I made for you.'

She held out a sweater. 'This is for you, Daddy. I love you so much.'

He embraced her gently and ruffled her hair. His wife came from the kitchen with a cup of coffee for him and noticed the sweater in his hand.

She asked, 'Is that yours?'

'Yes. Sabai made it for me. So sweet of her.'

She smiled, 'That's why the lights in her room stayed on long after midnight. She has been diligently knitting it for you.'

Sabai brought another sweater for her mother from her room, 'Mom, this is for you. I hope you like it. I love you too.' Her mother felt warmth inundate her heart when Sabai kissed her cheek.

They also visited a beach. One day, Sabai had said, 'Daddy, can we go to the beach after my exams?' He had promised that he would take her after her eighth standard examination.

At the beach, Sabai's parents looked on indulgently as their daughter enjoyed herself, drinking the water of tender coconuts, energetically running up and down on the seashore, swimming in the sea, riding her bicycle—in short, having a whale of a time, making the most of their little holiday.

After swimming in the sea, they all returned to the beach and gorged on fried fish. They watched the sunset together, enjoying the breeze. They trooped back to their hotel, where they had dinner and told each other stories before retiring to bed.

* * *

U Ba Win woke up, hearing a knock on the door. He opened it to see the young mother and her little son standing on their doorstep. She smiled and handed him a bowl, saying, 'It's fried chicken for you and Auntie.'

He thanked her and invited them in. Leading the mother and child into his wife's room, he gestured for them to sit in the chairs by his wife's bedside. He vanished into the kitchen and emerged a few minutes later with a tray holding a cup of coffee and some biscuits, placing it on the nightstand beside the bed. As the young mother and his wife chatted, he quietly left the room and returned to the living room.

U Ba Win tidied away the newspaper he had been reading and placed it on a shelf. Then, he looked for the books he had bought from the bookshop last Thursday when he had collected his pension. The new books were on the floor beside a stack of his collection of books.

Sitting in the armchair in his living room, he surveyed his little library. He decided that, someday, he would need to tidy it up and get rid of the books he didn't need—after all, there was no one in his family line to inherit them.

He sighed, contemplating the future. The previous night, he hadn't been able to get a wink of sleep. His wife had been coughing intermittently, and another thought that constantly nagged him was the way he and his wife continued to lead their lives after the departure of their dear daughter.

They had some relatives who were wholly unreliable and whom he didn't want to trouble. After all, these relatives had their own lives and families too. He wanted to handle his life in his own way. When the clock struck five in the morning, he made his decision.

* * *

He decided that he would sell everything—the furniture, the TV, his books, everything, and probably the apartment as well. He would divide the proceeds equally between him and his wife, don a yellow robe, and go to live in the monastery where his cousin and nephew lived. His wife could live out her days at the meditation centre.

He needed to run these plans by his wife. He was sure that she would agree with the idea.

* * *

Seated on the settee, he mentally drifted back fifty years when he had just been a young graduate working in a government office. He had enjoyed his job and had a passion for astrology as a hobby. Whenever he had a spare minute, he calculated the horoscopes for his peers pro bono, aiming to accumulate brownie points for good deeds.

It was during this period that he fell in love and married Tin. Unfortunately, there came a time when she suspected him of flirting with a woman who had come to discuss her horoscope with him. Tin grew jealous of her and uttered something bitter to him.

His wife's hurtful words, doubting his integrity, cut him like a sharp knife, piercing his heart. Later, out of pique, he stayed away and didn't go home regularly. To make her worried, he spent his nights at his friends' homes without telling her. Their relationship became strained until they had their daughter.

After Sabai came into their lives, U Ba Win settled down again as a family man and tried to heed his wife again. Their love resumed and they became a happy couple again. They agreed to raise their only daughter well and show her how good and capable they were as parents. They took pride in her and they intended to be dutiful parents.

* * *

One day, Sabai fell ill before she left for work. Not wanting to unnecessarily alarm her parents, she said nothing to them, thinking that she would shake it off and feel better soon. Later, she discovered that she had a serious disease, but she kept it a secret. The illness steadily worsened and claimed the young woman's life.

After their daughter's demise, their house became sombre and lifeless, like a desert.

U Ba Win's friends sent their condolences when they heard of his great loss. He was fatalistic about it and accepted it as the result of his past karma. He muttered, 'Everything is impermanent; nothing is permanent. Meeting will end in separation. It is the law of nature.'

* * *

His thoughts were interrupted when a cat leapt onto his chair
and purred. He patted it gently. The cat looked at him before
it leapt off the chair. At that instant, he made up his mind and
decided to carry through with his plan.

The young mother and her child came out of his wife's
room and smiled at him. He returned the smile and got up
from the settee to see them off at the door. She promised
to visit his wife often. He thanked the young woman. When
they left, he shut the door gently.

He went out to the veranda again and gazed at the sky,
observing a single heron winging its way towards the west.
It was probably going to forage in the paddy fields that lay
outside the town. He marvelled at the freedom of the heron's
life; it was quite different from his own. He knew that his life
would soon resemble the heron's after selling the house and
everything else he owned and settling things with his wife.
They both preferred to lead separate lives because they no
longer bonded.

He lived happily with his wife. Nevertheless, he needed
to prepare for the next phase in both his life and his wife's.
He wanted to provide her with space and freedom from the
constraints of marriage.

He looked for the heron in the sky, but couldn't find
it because it had already disappeared into the distance. He
walked quietly to the door of his wife's room and peeked in.
His wife was sound asleep. He decided to tell her his plan
when she woke up.

In the meantime, he went to the altar where the Buddha
image had been placed and prayed, reciting devotional texts.
The candle flickered in the breeze, casting shadows on the
wall that vaguely resembled his daughter's face. He shook his

head to dispel such fanciful notions because he knew very well that his daughter had transitioned to her next life. He visualized the image of the Buddha to grant him serenity.

After his prayers, he made a wish, 'I share with you the good merits I have accrued. Please accept them and you will be reborn on a pleasanter plane in which you will reap the benefits. *Sadhu, Sadhu, Sadhu* (well done).'

His voice echoed throughout the room along with the tinkling of a triangular copper bell that he struck on the edge with a wooden baton.

Gramarye

The moonless sky was pitch black and the nocturnal wind blew steadily as if an invisible fan had been switched on. He could hear the rustle of leaves in the nearby trees with every gust of the wind. The dim light caused the trees to cast elongated shadows in the streets.

The wind made rattling sounds as it swept discarded cans down the asphalt street. Parked cars under the street lamps seemed to be taking a break from their diurnal driving activities.

The intermittent howling of stray dogs in the distance made the dark night spookier. He tossed and turned in his bed, unable to sleep, reflecting on the incident that had occurred at the office. He felt bitter and cursed under his breath, 'Damn!'

He stood on the balcony, holding the balustrade and gazed around the environs. He beheld apartments in the neighbourhood; some of them plunged in darkness, while others still had their lights switched on. He noticed shadows moving behind the curtains. A newly-wed couple was dancing romantically in their room.

Living a solitary life as a bachelor, he envied them and their happiness. He inhaled the night air and tried to refresh his weary mind. That day, he had quarrelled with his colleague at work over a triviality.

He had noticed a curly-haired doll on his colleague's desk. Out of curiosity, and in the absence of his colleague, he had picked it up and had accidently knocked his colleague's coffee cup onto the carpeted floor.

At that very moment, his colleague emerged from the manager's office and yelled, 'Hey, how dare you touch my doll without my permission? Are you insane?'

He realized he was in the wrong, but being reprimanded in public felt demeaning, so he retorted, 'What's wrong with you? It's just a doll.' Saying that, he tossed the doll at his colleague who caught it immediately.

'You dare to treat it badly; you will regret this.'

'I don't care,' the protagonist replied, shaking his head as he tried to understand his colleague's oblique threat.

Thus, they had quarrelled. His colleague cursed him for his clumsiness and gave him a piece of his mind. The manager had to step in to stop the squabble from escalating into a pitched battle.

Just thinking about the incident raised his ire again. He shook his head to clear the ill feeling because he knew that hatred begets hatred. He needed to control his mind.

Just then, he heard a curious scratching sound at the front door. Faint at first, it grew louder after a while. At first, he ignored it, thinking that it would die down on its own.

But the sound grew persistent. He turned towards the door, his curiosity nudging him to find out what it was.

When he opened the door, he was surprised to see a black cat meowing loudly and pawing at the door with its claws. The cat seemed starved and hungry, and he felt a surge of pity for the poor creature.

He looked at the hall clock and noticed that it was almost 10.15 p.m. He knew that his neighbours were away on vacation and decided that he ought to feed their cat.

It turned around and around to demonstrate how tame it was. He went into the kitchen and luckily found some leftover bread from his own dinner.

He brought the bread along with a little bowl of milk to the cat who came running to door at the click of the doorknob.

He held the door ajar and placed the bread and the milk bowl on the threshold because he didn't want to allow the strange cat into his room. He thought that the cat would leave the premises as soon as it finishes its meal. He closed the door and let the cat enjoy its food in peace.

Unwilling to go to bed at this hour, he sat down on the couch in front of the TV and surfed the channels to see if he could find something interesting to watch. Whenever he found sleep evading him, he read a novel or watched a movie.

The TV screen's light flashed as it winked on and an old movie's title *Isabella* flickered on the screen. When he saw the name, he whispered it several times unconsciously. Instantly, he heard the raucous meowing of the cat.

Feeling a wee bit annoyed because he had just fed the cat, he wondered what it needed now, apart from more food.

He rose from the couch and yanked the door open to see what the hullaballoo was all about.

The meowing stopped abruptly and he assumed that the cat had left the place. Before he opened the door, he pressed his ear against the door to listen for the cat.

When he had assured himself that there was no sound, he opened the door. As soon as he opened it, he was unable to believe his eyes. In place of the cat, he saw a girl who was the spitting image of the doll with her long, curly hair and a black dress, standing in front of him.

A chill ran down his spine, goosebumps appeared on his limbs and his hair stood on end. He did his utmost, although unsuccessfully, to keep his composure. He reluctantly gazed into the girl's eyes and she held his stare without blinking.

Suddenly, immediately and uncontrollably his mouth started to move and he began to intone *meow, meow, meow* . . .

A Padauk Mission

A man named Tin Hla stared adoringly at the blooming padauk tree. In full bloom, with the sweet fragrance of its flowers wafting in the air, it was a spectacle to behold. He desperately wanted the padauk flowers because they would be the perfect solution to his romantic dilemma.

Moreover, padauk flowers always attract womenfolk when Thingyan comes around in April. The flowers are so fragrant that when they bloom, the air is heady with the perfume. The flowers normally need the pre-Thingyan fine rain to bloom fully.

Tin Hla was over forty years old, a bit bald, and in the habit of chewing betel. He was a bachelor and was seeking his soulmate earnestly. Then, he met Aye Mya, who was in her late twenties and a beautiful maiden. She came to live together with her aunt in Tin Hla's quarter in a Yangon suburb. As soon as Tin Hla saw her, he fell totally under the spell of her perfect beauty. She was fair-complexioned with long, black hair that were some of the most admired physical qualities in Myanmar women.

Tin Hla watched Aye Mya whenever she left home in the morning for a nearby wet market to buy groceries. Sometimes, he surreptitiously followed her. Actually, Aye Mya did notice this but she pretended she hadn't seen him. Sometimes, he waited for her at the corner of the street.

In fact, Tin Hla was looking for a chance to talk to her in person. Aye Mya was clever and knew exactly how to thwart his plans of approaching her. Unable to find a good opportunity to establish a friendship with her, Tin Hla grew disheartened. However, he still awaited the right moment to seize.

Luckily for him, one day, he was late to arrive at the corner of the street where he usually waited for her. He assumed that Aye Mya had already gone to the market.

He cursed his tardiness and sighed, 'Oh, I've missed the chance to see her. She must be already in the market by now.' Feeling depressed, he walked very slowly along the street leading to the market.

A few steps later, he saw an object, glittering in the sunlight. His curiosity aroused, he quickly looked around; no one seemed to have noticed him and he quickly picked it up. He saw that it was a gold bracelet with tiny heart talismans dangling from it. Amazed, he held it aloft to examine it against the sunlight.

Just then, Aye Mya suddenly appeared before him and snatched the bracelet from Tin Hla's hand. Tin Hla was shocked and angry. At first he thought how rude and obnoxious this person was, and he rolled up his sleeves, ready to reclaim the piece of jewellery forcefully. However, when he looked at the person, he saw the beaming face of Aye Mya.

'It's mine, a ko. I lost it on my way to the market. I'm so glad that it was you who found it. If I hadn't found it, my aunt would've scolded me severely. Thanks to you I don't have to worry about that. Thank you so much,' said Aye Mya pleasantly. As soon as he heard Aye Mya's words, Tin Hla's anger dissolved and he readily accepted her explanation.

'Really? Okay, take it, Aye Mya,' he stuttered.

Aye Mya thanked him prettily and invited him to accompany her to the market because she wanted to buy him a cup of tea as a token of her gratitude. Happily, Tin Hla walked alongside her.

Afterwards, they became friends. Later, he waited for her almost every morning and escorted her to the market and returned to their quarter together.

* * *

It had been a few months during which their friendship grew and burgeoned. In Tin Hla's mind, he was thinking of the right moment to tell Aye Mya how much his love for her had grown over the past few days. He realized that the Water Festival was approaching and decided to win her heart before the festival. Only then, they could happily participate in the festival.

He was aware that Aye Mya was rather shy and timid and that made it difficult for him to broach the topic of his love for her. As luck would have it, the previous day when he accompanied her to the market, Aye Mya had asked him to pick padauk flowers for her when she had seen the flowers blooming on the tree in their quarter.

In his mind, he decided that this was her test of his love for her. She might accept his suit if he could manage to pick the padauk flowers from the tree for her. It would also be a demonstration of his true love for her because he risked his life by climbing up the tall tree.

Aye Mya elaborated that she hadn't been able to find a suitable person to entrust this mission. Hearing these words, he felt elated and assured her that he would accomplish the task.

He also thought that he could not let slip such a golden opportunity to show her how capable and competent he was. Only the successful accomplishment of this quest— giving her the padauk flowers—would fulfil his dream of gaining her love.

When Aye Mya had finished telling him about her desire for the padauk flowers, Tin Hla promised, 'I'll return to our quarter now to get the flowers for you. I'll deliver them to your house and they'll be there when you return from the market.'

He hurried back to the quarter to pick the flowers as he had promised. When he arrived at the foot of the tree, he discovered to his dismay that the tree was alarmingly tall. His blood ran cold at the mere thought of climbing the giant tree, certain that such an endeavour would result in his falling to his death.

For several minutes, he stood dithering at the foot of the tree, not knowing what to do, and gazed longingly at the tantalizing flowers that seemed to mock him as they bloomed prolifically on the loftiest branches of the tree. It was a test of his courage to climb the tree. Perhaps the flowers knew of

his acrophobia and that he would not dare to climb to such a
height to pick them.

Tin Hla braced himself for this Herculean task. He could
not find a ladder or a bamboo post nearby and therefore got
ready to climb the tree the old-fashioned way—by using his
hands and feet to anchor himself. He slipped off his sandals
and placed them neatly at the foot of the tree. He hugged the
tree tightly with both arms and pressed the soles of his feet
against the trunk.

Two ravens, perched high up in the branches of a shady
tree nearby, scoffed at the ridiculous man who was trying to
climb a tree, 'Look at that silly fellow trying to pick padauk
flowers for a woman who is oblivious to his love for her.
What an ass!'

'True that. This man is a brainless ignoramus!'

A few minutes later they flew by. Although Tin Hla
painstakingly hauled himself up with concerted force, he
seemed to be making no progress at all. No matter how
hard he tried to scale the gigantic tree, gravity overpowered
him. Fortunately, he didn't plummet like a stone to earth. He
fastened himself to the tree like a human spider. Perspiration
beaded and then rolled down from his forehead. He was still
undecided about whether he should abort the mission or
not. An old saying entered uninvited into his worried head:
'Down until you touch the sand; up until you reach the top.'

Adrenaline and testosterone combined in his heart and
he did his utmost to extricate himself from his predicament.
However, the harder he tried, the faster he depleted his
strength. Finally, he had no choice but to abandon the attempt
as a lost cause. He had no clue about how he could get his
hands on this inaccessible prize.

At that instant, an idea struck him and he exclaimed at his good fortune. He saw a stone about ten feet away and quickly picked it up. He aimed it at the flowers and threw the rock with all his might. The stone was way off its mark the first time. He gasped with anguish and ran to pick up his missile again. He hurled it again towards the flowers dancing high in the boughs. This time again, luck was not on his side.

It was back to the drawing board.

His every attempt met with dismal failure. His heart sank and his head dropped. At this hopeless juncture, out of nowhere, the sweet smell of padauk flowers wafted into his nostrils. He looked around wondering where it came from.

Then he saw Poe Htaung, a boy of eight, walking towards him with some padauk flowers. A new idea struck him, and he stopped the boy. 'Hey, kid. Please, stop. Come over here,' he beckoned the lad.

The boy looked perplexed, but approached Tin Hla hesitantly. He beamed at the boy, who drew closer to Tin Hla because he seemed fairly harmless. Tin Hla whispered something to the boy, who nodded readily and handed over his flowers to Tin Hla.

A few minutes later, everyone in the ward saw Tin Hla standing at the gate of Aye Mya's house, holding a beautiful bunch padauk flowers.

'Aye Mya! Aye Mya! Here are some padauks for you.'

Aye Mya rushed out of the house smiling radiantly at him. She asked Tin Hla how he had managed to pick the padauk flowers. Tin Hla fabricated a fabulous tale of his perilous climb up the tree; it was a story of courage, endurance, and sacrifice. Aye Mya listened spellbound to the fairy tale. In his mind, Tin Hla secretly thanked Poe Htaung for selling him the padauk flowers on credit.

As everyone knows, luck is ephemeral. Tin Hla cringed upon hearing the humorous lyrics to Poe Htaung's satirical ditty as he strutted past Aye Mya's house:

'Tin Hla is such a coward,
He wouldn't dare climb a tree
Even worse, he lies through his teeth
Wouldn't you agree?'

A Bad Day

Myint Oo sat on the leather couch in his living room, plucking at the strings of his Yamaha hollow guitar. The tune sounded melodious, and he closed his eyes rapturously. After a few minutes, he scribbled down some music notes on a sheet of paper and set it aside for further development. Satisfied with the progress he had made, he returned the guitar to its stand and went into his bedroom.

He lived alone in his apartment on the third floor of a quiet downtown street. Now in his thirties, he dedicated his leisure time to composing songs as a form of self-expression.

Lying on his bed under a dim light, Myint Oo thought of his future. As a budding songwriter, he knew that he needed to showcase his lyrics and music to singers, but he didn't have any connections or a network to approach the vocalists. He sighed as he wondered how to overcome this impasse.

Myint Oo wrote songs especially meant for Myanmar stereo, which, as far as he was aware, had become popular in the 1970s. His compositions followed that style.

Locally, there were many famous Myanmar-stereo legends such as Sai Htee Saing, Khine Htoo, Khin Maung Toe, Soe Lwin Lwin, Htoo Eain Thin, and others. The local youth enjoyed the unique tonalities and styles of their songs. Most of their songs pioneered a new trend in music in those days, especially because Myanmar-stereo songs were very different from the genre of traditional Myanmar songs, locally known as 'mono songs'.

During a discussion about Myanmar-stereo music, some local music critics went so far as to say that the period between 1979 and 1989 was the golden age for Myanmar-stereo music.

Although he had played guitar ever since his high school days, Myint Oo had only just begun composing songs, drawing inspiration from those beautiful stereo songs. Due to several reasons, he had pursued other professions, forsaking his dream to become a lyricist. However, these days, the desire to compose had returned to him and he picked up the threads of his disconnected dream to try and materialize it.

To fulfil his dream, however, he needed someone who could put him in touch with singers because he was not in musical field per se, and he didn't have a circle of good friends in the music business. As a graphic designer, he had many friends, but they were all in various other fields.

* * *

One day, Myint Oo felt like tasting the tea in the new tea shop that had opened in his neighbourhood. He went there, sat down at a vacant table near the entrance of the tea shop and ordered a cup of tea. A bespectacled, middle-aged man asked his permission to share his table.

Myint Oo agreed, and the man sat down facing him. As they sipped their tea, the man kept stealing glances at him and it seemed like the man wanted to say something to him. Myint Oo smiled at him and the man returned his smile and started the conversation.

'I think I know you. Do you live around here?' asked the man.

'Yes, I live in this neighbourhood.'

Then, the man inquired, 'What do you do for a living?'

Myint Oo replied, 'I'm a graphic designer by profession and write songs as a hobby.'

The man seemed impressed and excited. 'Songs? What kind of songs? How many songs have you written?'

'I write stereo songs—slow rock, blues, etc. I've composed almost thirty songs already, but I need to show them to vocalists so they can sing my compositions.'

The gentleman nodded, 'If you'd like to show your songs to singers, perhaps I could help you. I know some of them. I used to work in a music store and I often meet them at bars.'

This sounded like a golden opportunity for Myint Oo. He replied, 'Yes, please, I'd like that very much.' He hoped that this kind gentleman would introduce him to some good vocalists. If they liked Myint Oo's compositions, they would buy his lyrics. Myint Oo's career as a songwriter would thus be launched, and there would be no turning back for him.'

He hoped that the man could be his liaison to famous and talented singers. He couldn't help smiling inwardly as the flickering flame of hope suddenly burned strong in his heart. He did not realize that the man was staring at him. The man gulped down some tea in the cup before pouring the green tea into a small cup.

The man continued, 'If you're free tomorrow, please come to this tea shop at 9.30 in the morning. One of the popular singers whom I know is due to attend the inauguration of the art exhibition. I'd like you to accompany me, because he has invited me to come. I can introduce you to him.'

'Thank you, sir. I will be here tomorrow morning.' Myint Oo paid the bill for both cups of tea, and they left the tea shop.

* * *

The next morning, Myint Oo woke up early and got ready for the appointment. He waited by the telephone for the man's call at around nine in the morning to confirm their rendezvous at the tea shop. In the meanwhile, he received an urgent call from his relative, who kept him talking for about twenty minutes. He realized that he had several missed calls when he eventually hung up.

The missed calls were from his new benefactor. Myint Oo immediately returned his call, but the man's phone was busy. Out of patience, Myint Oo got ready to go to the tea shop to keep his appointment. On the verge of leaving home, he dialled the man's number one last time.

The gentleman answered his phone, 'I called you several times, but you failed to answer your phone. I've already left for the exhibition with my other friends in their van. You can come down directly to the exhibition hall and I'll meet you there.'

* * *

Myint Oo quickly changed his clothes and left to grab a taxi to the exhibition. The cabbie dropped him to the exhibition venue in less than twenty minutes.

Myint Oo hurriedly paid the fare and alighted. He found himself in a pleasant, spacious compound with large trees. The atmosphere was serene. He knew that in its vicinity there was a renowned art school that also served as a cultural centre.

He headed to the exhibition building. The hall already had quite a few people paying close attention to an aged artist conducting his artistic demonstration. A lovely lady in a Burmese dress and a sophisticated hairdo was modelling a food holder in her hand.

He looked around at the lovely paintings and enjoyed the exhibition, but in his mind, he was waiting impatiently for the famous vocalist to arrive. He frequently checked the time on his watch. He telephoned the gentleman who had invited him here and when he eventually answered his call, he said that he was on his way to another suburb with his friends and would be back in thirty minutes.

* * *

After staring at the paintings for hours, Myint Oo grew bored and decided to go outside for some fresh air. He waited for a long time in front of the building, and watched other visitors and viewers come and go with their friends and colleagues. To kill time, he looked at his phone and scrolled through some pictures he had clicked.

From time to time, he craned his neck to peer into the driveway, checking whether his sponsor had arrived. There was still no sign of either the sponsor or the famous vocalist. Although Myint Oo wasn't sure about this, he assumed that it was quite possible that the vocalist would arrive later that day or in the afternoon.

Finally, after waiting for an hour, Myint Oo concluded that his sponsor had let him down and wouldn't come. On their last telephone conversation, the gentleman had said that he would arrive in a few minutes. Myint Oo grumbled under his breath to himself doubting the reliability of the man's words.

He smiled sadly, wallowing in self-pity. He had been utterly naïve to believe a person he had just met and he mentally kicked himself for his gullibility. He sighed and prepared to head for a bus stop nearby to catch a bus home.

Looking up at the overcast sky, he decided that it had been an all-round bad day for him and that he ought to regard it as a life lesson in his new career. 'Phew!' he sighed gustily.

Then, he slowly directed his steps towards the bus stop where other commuters were also waiting for a bus.

Acknowledgements

These stories are the output of my writing in the span of a decade between 2010 and 2020. During this time, I met people and worked in different journals and magazines such as *Home and Services Journal, Learners' Educative Magazine, My Yangon Magazine, Myanmore, Myanmar Times,* etc.

Some editors asked me to write interesting stories on Yangon including people and places on a regular basis. So, I ventured out to the city life. But my interest was more in ordinary people and their lives. So I had a chance to write stories about them in different literary forms such as flash fiction, vignettes, and short stories.

Accordingly, some stories have appeared in local magazines and international platforms. Some haven't found their home yet. It had been my intention to compile all these stories into a short story collection. And now it's materialized with this publication with Penguin SEA that is one of the leading and prestigious publishers in the region.

I would like to express my sincere thanks to the following: Sayardaw (Venerable) U Sasanapala, my mentor who instilled the habit of reading in me; Sayar Lay Ko Tin, my senior writer who encourages me to write in English; Lucas Stewart and Zee, who support me in my writing career; Keith Lyons, who has been with me in my writing profession since we are friends; Cristina and George, who bring books for me during their visit to Yangon; Jonathan, who likes to walk Yangon streets with me; Iris Frei, who shows encouragement whenever my books come out; Jim Hayton, who is ready to be a host for my literary event; Tatwin, Emily, John, Andrew, who are my former editors; Don, who asks me to co-author his book; and John for his caring friendship. Moreover, my wife, Nwe, my two sons, Tun and Kyaw, my siblings, in-laws, and especially editors and team at Penguin SEA, and those who are in my literary circle, etc. Without their unfailing help and support, this book would not have seen the light of day.